"Are you only helping me because you feel sorry for me?"

Bob gazed into Georgette's blue eyes. Of course he felt badly about the way her father had rejected her, because she wanted to build a life of her own. Actually, he felt proud of her, too.

And yet, he didn't feel at peace with what was happening between them.

Until now, Georgette hadn't had to work. She could have lived a life of leisure, and it wouldn't have been wrong.

But now, all that was gone.

That a working-class guy like him could be her employer was one of life's cruel jokes. For now, having to work and save money to get what she wanted, and even the necessities of daily life, was a novelty. Very soon, that thrill would wear off....

Falling in love with someone from the other side of the tracks only worked in romance novels and fairy tales.

Books by Gail Sattler

Love Inspired

Hearts in Harmony #300
His Uptown Girl #309

*Men of Praise

GAIL SATTLER

lives in Vancouver, British Columbia (where you don't have to shovel rain), with her husband of twenty-six years, three sons, two dogs, five lizards, one toad and a Degu named Bess. Gail loves to read stories with a happy ending, which is why she writes them. Visit Gail's Web site at www.gailsattler.com.

HIS UPTOWN GIRL

GAIL SATTLER

Steeple
Hill®

Published by Steeple Hill Books™

STEEPLE HILL BOOKS

Steeple
Hill®

ISBN 0-373-87319-0

HIS UPTOWN GIRL

Copyright © 2005 by Gail Sattler

This edition published by arrangement with Steeple Hill Books.

® and TM are trademarks of Steeple Hill Books, used under license. Trademarks indicated with ® are registered in the United States Patent and Trademark Office, the Canadian Trade Marks Office and in other countries.

www.SteepleHill.com

Printed in U.S.A.

He gives strength to the weary
and increases the power of the weak.
—*Isaiah* 40:29

Dedicated to my husband, Tim.
Just because I love you.

———

Chapter One

The electronic tone of the door chime echoed through the shop.

Bob Delanio laid his wrench down on the tool caddy, wiped his hands on his coveralls, then walked into the reception area of his auto-repair shop.

"Need some help?" he asked his newest customer, trying not to sound as tired as he felt.

The phone rang. Both lines lit up at the same time.

"Oops, 'scuse me," Bob mumbled as he picked up the receiver. "Bob And Bart's, can you hold?" He pushed the button and answered the second line. "Bob And Bart's. Yeah. Hold on." Bob hit the hold button, walked a few steps, and poked his head around the corner.

"Bart!" he yelled. "Get line two. It's Josh McTavish."

Bob nodded at the man still waiting at the counter. The chime sounded again. Just as Bob picked up the phone to talk to the first caller, a man who a week ago had ignored Bob's warning that he needed a new head gasket stomped in. Bob glanced through the door to see a tow truck outside, the driver waiting to be told what bay to back the man's car into.

Bob gritted his teeth. It appeared he was going to spend yet another Friday night working until midnight.

He handled the latest influx, then did his best to juggle his time between the door, the phone, and actually getting some work done.

At seven o'clock, an hour past their posted closing, Bart finally had the time to flip the switch on the sign on the door to Closed. Despite that positive turn, neither of them would be leaving just yet.

"This is nuts," Bart grumbled as he dropped some change into the pop machine for a cold drink. "We can't keep this up."

Falling backwards onto the worn couch, Bob stretched out his aching feet. "I know. It's great that business is picking up, but I'm exhausted." He extended one arm toward the unfinished work orders lined up on the board. "No matter what time we get out of here, we'll have to be back at five in the morning."

"My wife isn't very pleased about these long hours. At least you're still single," Bart retorted.

"Maybe this is why I'm still single."

Bart turned to look outside at the row of cars they had promised their customers they could pick up sometime within the next twenty-four hours. "We have to hire some help."

The growing pile of invoices and purchase orders on the counter, spurred Bob's reply. "I was just thinking the same thing."

Bart turned and walked behind the counter. He grabbed a blank piece of paper and pulled a pen out of his pocket. "The newspaper charges by the word, don't they? What should I say? Wanted. Light-duty mechanic?"

Without leaving the couch, Bob scanned the boxes of orders, requisitions, receipts and charge bills to be submitted, as well as deposit slips from the bank. "We're busy, but we're not busy enough to add another full-time mechanic. If we hire a bookkeeper, then that frees us up to get more done in the shop."

Bart scratched his head, pen in hand. "But there are decisions a bookkeeper can't make, stuff one of us would have to decide. Besides, we don't have enough paperwork to keep someone busy full-time. When all this stuff is caught up, we can't afford to pay someone just to sit here and answer the phone."

"We're nearly a week behind even on the small jobs," Bob said, gesturing at the work orders piled under push-pins on their work board. "I've got an overhaul that's been waiting three days. I guess you're right. We need a mechanic."

Bart stuck his hand in the closest box and lifted out a handful of papers. "It's almost our fiscal year-end, time for our corporate taxes. Your friend Adrian always needs everything balanced, reconciled and printed out so he can file for us. You're right. We need a bookkeeper."

The two men stared at each other in silence.

"We need both," Bob mumbled, "But it would be too hard to hire two part-timers. I don't want to invest all our time and money to train someone, then have them quit for a better job elsewhere that can give them more hours when they get enough experience. Maybe we should forget about it."

Bart shook his head. "The baby is three weeks old. I never see her except when she's up in the middle of the night crying. And that's when I should be sleeping, too. I can't keep this up."

Bob felt his whole body sag. Neither of them could continue working eighteen-hour days, six days a week. Lately, the only time Bob wasn't working was when he took off a few hours Wednesday evening to practice the songs he would be playing on Sunday with his church's worship team. Up until recently, he refused to work Sundays, but they were so far behind, he'd started to work a few hours on Sunday, too.

He didn't know when control had first eluded them, but they'd reached their breaking point. Soon they were going to start making mistakes, which, where cars and people were concerned, could not happen.

It had to stop.

"You're right. We both need to slow down. Let's hire two part-timers, a mechanic and a bookkeeper, and we'll see what happens." The stack of work orders lined up for Saturday, was well beyond what they could accomplish, even if both he and Bart worked twenty-four hours nonstop.

Dropping his pen suddenly as if at a thought, Bart turned to the computer. "I just remembered something. I don't have to write out that ad. I heard that you can do it online. I can even put it on my charge card."

Bob stood. "You've probably missed the deadline for tomorrow's paper."

Bart found the right Website, and started typing in his usual hunt-and-peck, two-finger mode. "Maybe I haven't."

Suddenly Bob's head swam as the magnitude of the process hit him. "I just thought of something. What about all the phone calls, and the time it's going to take to set up and do interviews?"

Bart's fingers stilled. "What are you trying to say?"

"We don't have that kind of time. People are going to start taking their business elsewhere."

"Have you got a better idea?"

Bob walked to the counter, and reached for one of the boxes containing incomplete purchase orders. He tore off the flap to the box, picked up the black felt pen, and began to write.

HELP WANTED—APPLY WITHIN
Part-time light-duty mechanic
Part-time office assistant
Hours and wages negotiable.

He dug a roll of black electrical tape out of the drawer while Bart watched, and taped the cardboard to the window.

"What are you doing?"

Bob turned around. "Saturday is our busiest day, and lots of people come in. If any of them are interested, we can take care of interviewing right there. We should forget about the ad."

"You're kidding, right?"

Bob raised his hand toward the sign, which was slightly crooked. "Do I look like I'm kidding?"

"I guess you're really not kidding," Bart mumbled.

Bob sighed. The business had supported both him and Bart for years, and now there was also Bart's family. They couldn't fail now. There was too much at stake.

"God will provide," Bob said softly. I've always believed in God's timing, and I still do."

Bart resumed his typing. "You're crazy. Certifiably crazy."

Bob spun around. "Don't you believe God can send us the right people?"

"I doubt God will have the right people simply fall from the sky. But I do know one thing. If we don't get McTavish's 4X4 finished, we'll be in trouble when he comes to get it at 7:00 a.m. I'm putting this ad in the paper. I'm sure God will have the right people fax in their résumés."

"I still think we'll do better with the sign in the window. We don't have the time or the energy for millions of faxes and phone calls. Besides, there's more to hiring than just looking at résumés."

"But that's where we have to start, and the only way we're going to get qualified people to send us those résumés is through the paper." Bart hit Enter. "Done. The ad's in."

Bob crossed his arms over his chest and turned his head to look at his sign. "And the sign is up. It looks like the battle is on."

Bart killed the browser. "Yeah. May the best man win. Now let's get back to work."

"Daddy! This dress is horrible!"

Georgette Ecklington's father flashed her a condescending smile. "The girl at the store told me you would look great in it."

Georgette gritted her teeth and pressed her lips together so hard they hurt. The "girl" in question was thirty-five years old. Because her father was one of their best customers and always paid full price, the woman happily told him anything he wanted to hear.

Still, the woman was probably right. Georgette knew she would look "good" in yet another overly frilly, fussy, pink dress with enough lace to choke a horse. If that was the way she wanted to look.

Which she didn't.

"Don't disappoint me, Georgie-Pie." Her father's stern gaze belied the familiarity of the nickname.

Georgette stifled a scream. She hadn't been five years old for twenty years, but whenever her father wanted something, he called her the childish nickname to remind her of something she could never forget.

She was William Ecklington's daughter.

And William Ecklington was in control. Always.

He'd picked that particular moment to give her another dress she hated because the household staff were in earshot. She couldn't disobey his orders in front of the staff or any of his peers. He would never forgive her for any act of defiance, or anything that might diminish his public image.

Tonight, at yet another Who's Who function, Georgette was expected to stand at her father's side and smile nicely, showing her support of everything he did. Besides his financial empire, the next most important thing to her father was the respect of his peers. After her mother had left him, he'd refused to marry again. He never dated because he was certain that women were only after his money. So, his younger daughter became second-best.

Georgette's only escape from her father's tyranny would be to do what her sister had done—to get married. But God said that marriage was forever. Georgette didn't want to be under the thumb of a man who was a younger version of her father—a man so critical and demanding he had driven their mother away. Her influential father also sabotaged every attempt she made to find a job, completely nullifying all her attempts to become independent. Not that she needed to worry about money, he gave her a generous allowance in exchange for her work on his charity projects. But Georgette wasn't happy.

"Be ready at five-fifteen. Karl will be driving." With that lofty pronouncement, her father turned and left.

Georgette crumpled the dress in her closed fists, and raised her head to the ceiling in a silent prayer. She needed to escape, and she had only one place to go, the only place her father left her alone.

The garage. The garage was her haven. Some women made crafts or baked when they needed something to do. Rebuilding an engine was Georgette's respite from "society." She detested being involved with the social climbing of her father's shallow world.

Working on the car, she didn't have to be Georgette Ecklington, socialite. She could simply be, as her friends at the pit crew of the local racetrack circuit called her, George. Today it would help her prepare herself for the ordeal of another taxing night.

She walked out of the room and handed the dress to Josephine, the housekeeper. "This needs pressing. I have some shopping to do, and then I need to be left alone until it's time to get dressed."

Josephine smiled and nodded. Josephine often covered for Georgette when her father was looking for her.

Soon Georgette was on her way to an out-of-the-way, but spectacular, auto shop she'd discovered, where the owners frequently found salvaged items from auto wreckers for her. She needed parts for her current project—restoring an old pickup truck she'd bought from one of the families in her church. The man had lost his job and the family needed money. They wouldn't accept charity, so instead, Georgette had bought the family's derelict pickup truck for many times more than it was worth, a sum that would keep their mortgage at bay for at least six months. She was now working to restore the truck. Perhaps someday the thing would even run again.

As she pulled into the shop, Georgette formulated her priorities. In three hours she had to be showered and ready, so she needed to make good use of her time.

Her thoughts cut off abruptly when she approached the store and saw a cardboard sign in the window.

HELP WANTED.

Georgette's breath caught. She quickened her pace, able to read the smaller print when she stood beside the door.

Light-duty mechanic.

She could do that. Fixing and rebuilding engines might just be a hobby, but she did it well. The pros at the race track confirmed it again and again. She'd never tackled a project she couldn't complete. And unlike the other times her father had ruined her job chances with a phone call, her references could be her friends at the race track. Her father didn't even know about this place, not that he'd deign to go to an auto shop any way. Georgette said a short prayer that they wouldn't ask for more, and pushed the door open.

The phone was ringing, and two customers waited impatiently ahead of her. Bob was behind the counter, taking notes as a woman listed the problems with her car. The voice of Bart, the other proprietor, echoed from the shop, over the noise of the hydraulic hoist, as he called for another customer to come out. Help certainly was wanted at Bob And Bart's Auto Repair.

While she waited for her turn, Georgette watched Bob a little more closely. Even though she'd been there before, she'd paid more attention to the spectacular finds he'd made for her than what either of the men looked like.

He carried himself with confidence as he dealt with his customers. Considering his job, he was relatively tidy in appearance, although his dark hair could use a cut. His olive-green eyes and Roman nose made her suspect an Italian heritage, though, the poster on the wall advertising a discount at Bob's brother's Italian restaurant, was a pretty solid hint, too.

As she stepped ahead in the line, she continued to study Bob.

He was a good-looking man. When he smiled, the hint of crow's feet at the corners of those amazing eyes put him at thirtyish.

After a short conversation, the man ahead of her followed Bob to the opening between the lobby and the shop. Bob called out to Bart, left the man where he was, then returned to his place behind the counter. "Can I help you?" Bob asked as he reached for a blank work order. As he turned to her, his frown turned to a small smile. "Right. I left a message on your cell phone. Your parts are in. I'll go get them. What's your name again?"

Georgette's stomach quivered. "Ecklington. George Ecklington."

His smile widened. "Of course. George. How could I forget? I'll be right back."

"No! Bob! Wait!" Georgette called as he took his first step away.

When he turned back to her, she cleared her throat. "Yes, I'm here for my parts, but I see you're hiring. I'd like to apply for the job."

His smile widened even more. He pulled an application from beneath the counter and slid it toward her. "I didn't have time to make our own applications, so I borrowed a few from my brother. It says Antonio's Ristorante at the top, but just cross it out, and write Bookkeeper in the corner so I'll put it in the right pile."

Georgette tried not to let her annoyance show. She didn't want the bookkeeper's job. Usually she could understand when people in her father's circle treated her like a frail little tulip, but to Bob, she was a customer—a customer who frequently bought parts, and installed them. Herself. She didn't like his assumption, but she'd had to prove herself at the raceway, too.

However, it wasn't as if she couldn't do the bookkeeping. Having been confined to her father's charities, she'd picked up the skill, including receivables, purchasing and handling the disbursements. She could imagine her father's blood boiling at the thought of his daughter doing work that paid by the hour. But not a dime of the allowance he'd given her was truly hers.

This job and its salary, independent of her father, or of anyone who had any association with her father, would be.

Georgette looked up at Bob, trying to show more confidence than she felt. "Actually, I'd like to apply for both jobs."

"Pardon me?"

"I can do bookkeeping, but I'm also a light-duty mechanic. Your sign said the hours were negotiable. Could two part-time jobs add up to one full-time job?"

Bob's smile dropped. "I'm sorry, but we need a real mechanic, not just someone to change oil and check spark plugs."

"But I *am* a real mechanic. I usually do rebuilds, but there's no reason I couldn't work on current models."

"Well, maybe you could, but I don't think—"

As she pictured herself actually working there, the things she knew she could do bubbled in her mind. "When people come in and they don't know what's wrong, if you just hired a bookkeeper, you'd have to stop what you were doing and listen to them. If you hired me, I would get a pretty good idea of what was wrong right off the bat, even if I wasn't the one to do the actual work."

Bob raised one finger in the air. "But—"

Her words tumbled over his protest. "Then you'd have the option of being able to use me in the shop or the office, wherever I was more needed at the time. Or I could—"

Bob put up his hands. "That really wasn't what we had in mind."

She narrowed her eyes. "Are you saying a woman couldn't do this job?"

"No! That's not what I'm saying at all…"

"I might be a woman, but I'm a good mechanic, and that's what you're hiring. I would do a good job for you. For *both* positions. I could even start Monday."

"Monday? Really…?" Bob's voice trailed off. He closed his eyes, and pinched the bridge of his nose. "Bart and I never discussed this possibility. We have to think about it. Why don't you fill out the application, and when you're done I'll call him in here so we can talk about it?"

Georgette tried to calm her racing heart. It was a possibility. Thoughts of her father's vehement disapproval slammed into her, but she pushed them aside. If Bob offered her the job, she would come up with a way to deal with her father. She couldn't think of anything she wanted more than this job.

The chime sounded behind her as another customer walked in. Georgette slid to the end of the counter to fill out the application, using her race track friends as references, though she had to list her father's holding company as current employer.

When she finished writing, she waited for Bob to complete the work order for his current customer whom she could hear describing the problem he was having with his car.

After the man left, Georgette spoke up. "It's the coil," she said. "Sounds faulty."

"You think so? I was just thinking the same thing."

Before she could respond, Bart walked into the lobby, wiping his hands on the back of his coveralls. "You here for the office job?" he asked.

Bob glanced at Bart, then back to Georgette. "You may not believe this, but she's here for both jobs." He handed Bart her application along with the newest work order. "Pull this one into bay four. If it's the coil that's causing the problem, we just might have found ourselves a new mechanic. And bookkeeper. Bart, this is George."

One of Bart's eyebrows raised. "George?"

She stiffened. "It's short for Georgette. My friends call me George."

He scanned the application, and gave a slight nod when he saw her racetrack references. "This is good. I know Jason from the track. I'll talk to him. But I know I've seen you somewhere before. Do you go to Faith Community Fellowship?"

Georgette shook her head. "No. I attend a church nearer to my house. I don't live nearby. But I buy most of my parts here."

"Must be it." Bart walked back to bay four with Bob.

Her heart pounded as she watched them check her assessment, nodding as they discussed the faulty coil.

When they returned to the lobby, she couldn't hold back any more. "Was I right?"

"Looks like it. As soon as Bart puts a new coil in and test drives it, he's going to watch the front desk so you and I can go into the office and discuss the details. You said Monday is good?"

"Monday is great." She marveled at her calm tone. "But I want to do my first official duty right now."

One eyebrow quirked.

Without waiting for him to respond, Georgette turned, walked to the cardboard sign in the window, and flipped it into the garbage can.

She had a job. A real job. And she'd done it without her father.

Chapter Two

The early-morning spring breeze drifted into the shop, doing its best to combat the smells of gas, oil and lubricants.

Bob had just reached down to check the power-steering belt of the car he was working on when an expensive sports car with tinted windows stopped in front of the bay next to him and began to back in.

Bob straightened, wiped his hands on the rag from his pocket, and watched the door to the car open.

A sleek, spike-heeled shoe poked out, followed by a slender, shapely leg. A swish of soft fabric brought the flow of a skirt, followed by the rest of the beautiful blond driver.

"Hi, Bob. I brought my tools. Where should I put them?"

Bob's heart pounded. He stared openly at his new mechanic. If she hadn't spoken, he wouldn't have recognized her, she was always so casually dressed the other times she'd come into the shop with her blond hair tied up in a ponytail, probably an attempt to make herself appear taller. Today, George wore makeup and a hairstyle fit for a magazine cover. Her outfit was nicer than most women he knew wore for special occasions. It was probably more expensive as well.

He didn't want or need a fashion model. He needed someone who could change a head gasket.

Bob wondered if he'd made his decision to hire her too impulsively. He tried to think of how to tell her that maybe he would have to reconsider, when George reached into the car, pulled out a duffel bag, and slung it over her shoulder. "I'll be right back. I have to change into something more suitable before I start working."

Before he could think of a response, she dashed off, the click of her high heels echoing against the concrete as she ran.

Bob checked his watch. It was fifteen minutes before her agreed start time. If he told her he'd changed his mind before she actually started, that might not count as actually firing her. It would probably be less painful that way.

She reappeared in minutes in comfortably worn jeans, a T-shirt proclaiming the tour of a popular Christian musician, and appropriate steel-toed safety boots. Turning as she spoke, she tossed the duffel into the back seat of her car. "I didn't know if you had coveralls that would fit me, so I brought my own. I hope that's okay."

"Uh…yeah…"

Bob shook his head to clear it. At least he would see what she could do. "Ready?"

"Soon as I unpack my tools. They're in the trunk."

Bob turned to stare at her car, which was probably worth at least triple the sticker price of his. "Nice," he said, positive she'd been driving something else when she'd applied for the job. He couldn't see why someone who could afford such a car would apply at his simple shop, she was obviously used to living on more money than he could pay.

"This car does tend to turn heads. It's my father's."

Bob's father had never owned such a car. And if he had, Bob knew he would never get to borrow it.

She pushed the remote button on her keychain. The trunk popped open to display a neat array of good-quality tools packed neatly in two boxes.

"I wasn't sure what to bring, so I brought just the basics."

Bart chose that moment to appear. He immediately walked to the car and picked up George's power wrench testing the heft with visible appreciation.

"Do you have a tool caddy for me?"

"We've got four bays," Bob answered. "Since you're the one who's going to be answering the phone most of the time, you take Bay One, which is closest to the lobby. Put your tools in the shelving unit on the wall over there."

In only minutes they had George's tools packed away in the appropriate place.

Bart stood beside Bob as George moved her car away. "I hope we're not taking this 'trusting God' thing a little too far."

"I don't know. All day yesterday at church, I kept thinking that God was sending us someone who really needed the job, but obviously she doesn't. I wonder if this is some kind of test."

Bart shook his head. "Let's not ask for more trouble. If nothing else, she'll look good when customers come in. Too bad she took her hair down and wiped off her makeup. Yowsa."

Bob stiffened. "I won't resort to the trick of hiring only pretty girls, like some of the places that deliver parts. I hired her because she immediately identified that coil problem."

"Okay, she knows something about mechanics. But can she balance a spreadsheet? Did you notice that she only had those track references? It probably would have been a good idea to check out her former employer, but that would have made things difficult for her if they hadn't known she was interviewing. Anyway, now it's too late."

"There's only one way to find out what she's like. Let's get her started."

Bart shook his head. "I don't have time to show her anything. They're coming to get that red sedan in an hour, and I'm not sure I'll be finished. You hired her, so you train her."

Bart walked off before Bob could respond.

Bob entered the lobby at the same time as George.

"Where do I start?" she asked.

"I guess the first step is to enter all the purchase orders into the computer," Bob said as he led her to the shop's computer. "We've kind of been letting it slip. When we're so busy, the paperwork is the last thing to be done. It drives our accountant nuts. Fortunately he's a friend."

He showed her how to enter a few transactions. "Write the journal entry number on everything as you enter it, and then put them in that box. I take the box home once a month just so everything will be in a separate location if anything happens."

She nodded as she entered a new purchase order. "This is a good program. I've used it before."

Bob stood back and watched her work. She entered everything quickly and with obvious proficiency, and her skill got him to thinking.

On Saturday, she'd appeared more the tomboy type, especially since she claimed to be a competent mechanic. But today, after seeing her grace and refinement when she came in, and now her bookkeeping skills, he was riveted to her every movement.

He watched as she paused in figuring out how to handle a difficult transaction. When she found the correct category for the particular part, she smiled to herself, and kept typing.

As she started to reach for another piece of paper out of the box, the phone rang.

Her hand froze in midair. "Should I get that?"

"Yep, that's another reason you're here."

She grinned and picked up the phone. "Good morning, thank you for calling Bob And Bart's Auto Repair. How may I direct your call?"

Bob dragged his hand down his face.

"One moment, please," she chirped, then pressed the hold button. "Larry Holt wants to know if his car is ready, and how much it will be."

"This isn't an executive office. You can say 'good morning' if you want, but we just say 'Bob 'n' Bart's' without having to make a speech about it. Things are pretty simple here. Tell Larry his car will be ready at two, and we're not sure how much yet until we know if we have to replace the ignition switch. And try to be less formal."

Her face reddened. She finished the call, then returned to the entry on the computer.

At the sight of that attractive blush, Bob decided to

linger a bit, just in case she had questions. He had wondered what it would be like to have another person around, especially a woman. He'd never had an employee before. Bart and he had been friends long before they became business partners, and it was only their friendship and their shared faith in God that sustained them through the hard times.

This was different. George was an attractive woman and Bart was, well, Bart. But George was also his employee, and no more. He'd often heard not to mix business with pleasure, and this was definitely one of those times. It was his decision to hire her, and conversely, if she messed up, it would be his responsibility to fire her.

He didn't want to think of firing her when she'd been there less than an hour. He wanted to give her a chance to prove what she could do.

He cleared his throat. "I'm going to get back to work now. If you need help, just call and one of us will come."

George frowned at the computer and looked up at him. "There's an awful lot of stuff not entered. I'm okay for now, but the true test will be when I have to do the monthly reconciliations. You do reconcile monthly, don't you?"

"Uh… We try, but not always. Anyway, we'd like you to do the paperwork in the morning, then after lunch you'll work in the shop. We need you to get right into routine today."

She smiled. "Of course. While I don't mind the paperwork, remember, it's the mechanic's job I applied for first."

Bob stared at her face, which held nothing but sincerity, trying to make sense of her. While he'd met a few women who could tell an alternator from a fuel pump, he didn't know many who were willing to touch them, much less actually change them.

"I'll leave you alone, then. Call me if you need anything."

She nodded, and Bob walked into the shop to finish his own work.

The morning moved more slowly for him than any other morning in the history of their business. It didn't help that he kept looking through the glass partition between the shop and the office to see how George was doing.

Just as she had when he was beside her, George appeared to be doing fine without him.

The real test would be when lunch break was over, and the second phase of her duties began.

Georgette looked up at the clock. Right on time, Bob walked into the lobby.

"I'm back. It's time for your lunch break, and then I'll get you started on a few tune-ups and things."

Georgette folded her hands on the countertop. "Actually, I ate my lunch as I worked. I hope that's okay." Her father would have died to think that she'd eaten while standing at the counter, as people came in and out. However, with all the excitement of doing something new, and running back and forth between the shop and the phone all morning, she'd been hungry an hour before it was technically lunchtime.

It was actually kind of fun, breaking the rules.

"I hope you don't think we mean for you to work through your lunch break, because we don't. If you've already eaten, would you like to go for a walk or something? There's a place down the block that has great ice cream cones. It's opened early because of our great May weather." The second the words were out of his mouth, he paused as if to gauge her response.

Georgette broke into a smile. She couldn't remember the last time she'd had the simple pleasure of eating an ice cream cone, or any kind of ice cream that wasn't a part of a fancy dessert, meant to impress. Her father didn't think ice cream cones were very dignified.

She reached under the counter for her purse. "I'd love an ice cream. How long will we be gone?"

"We? I… Uh…" Bob looked up at the clock, then shrugged his shoulders. "I hadn't intended for any of us to take our breaks at the same time, but we can probably make an exception for your first day. Just a sec." He turned and walked the three steps to the door leading to the shop, and opened it. "Bart!" he hollered. "I'm taking George for an ice cream down the street! We'll be back in twenty!"

Bob didn't wait for a reply. "Let's go while things are quiet. This doesn't happen often."

He shucked his coveralls off, pressed a few crinkles out of his jeans and T-shirt with his hands, and met her at the door.

"What about the phone?"

"Bart will do the same thing we've always done. He'll keep working, and when the phone rings, he'll go answer it."

"It's really nice that you don't ignore your calls and let them go to voice mail."

Bob nodded. "When we've got someone's car, they don't want to talk to a machine. They want an answer from a person, even if it's an 'I don't know.' I feel the same way when I'm calling for status."

Georgette thought of her father's charity. Only people who wanted to ingratiate themselves with him called. They found leaving a message more efficient.

She hated dealing with the machine because she missed the personal contact. On the other hand, the way everything was handled now suited her well. She'd told her father that she could handle the organization's details in the evening, since it only took an hour each day, and she never talked to anyone, anyway. This left her free to seek out something else to do during the daytime. He wasn't pleased she had found something now, but didn't press her for details probably figuring it wouldn't last.

As they crossed the intersection, Bob pointed to the north. "There's a small mall down that way, if you ever need anything. Next door to the mall are a couple of fast-food places." He jerked his head in the opposite direction, toward the residential area. "But if you want one of the best corned beef on rye sandwich in the world, there's a neighborhood market down that way."

"It sounds like you know the area really well."

Bob smiled. Little crinkles appeared in the corners of his eyes. His whole face softened, confirming her earlier opinion that her boss was quite a good-looking man.

"I grew up here. The reason Bart and I chose the location is because most of our initial customers were people we knew. It's worked well, so we're still here."

As they walked, they passed a number of specialty stores and small office buildings in the small commercial district. Not a single building was over two stories tall, and there were actually open metered parking spots on the street. The ambience of the district was nothing like the hustle and bustle of downtown. Georgette liked it.

By the time they arrived at the ice cream shop, Georgette could feel effect of the unaccustomed weight of the steel-toed safety boots on her lower back, far different from too-high high heels. Thinking of her closet-full of spike heels, and the shoes she'd worn earlier, she inwardly shuddered at the thought of forcing her feet back into such things to go home.

"What flavor do you want?"

Georgette stared up in awe at the board listing the flavors.

She probably could have picked an old standard, but today was a day of new experiences. Today was her first day of independence. Therefore, she wanted to pick the wildest flavor she could.

She tipped her head toward Bob and whispered, "What's Tiger Tiger?"

He pointed to a bin containing swirls of black and orange stripes. "I've had that before. It's a little strange. Orange and licorice. My favorite is the Chocolate Chip Cookie Dough."

She didn't care if it was strange. She wanted to have an ice cream flavor she'd never had before, to celebrate her first day of doing a job she'd never done before.

She turned to the kid behind the counter. "I'll have the Tiger Tiger, please."

When the clerk began scooping the bright colors into a huge waffle cone Georgette reached to open her purse, but Bob stopped her.

"No, this is my treat. In honor of your first day."

"Really?"

Bob smiled and turned to the clerk. "And the usual for me. Thanks." He paid the teenager.

Georgette didn't know how to respond. Of course it was only a simple ice cream cone, an inexpensive treat, but no one had ever given her anything when her father hadn't been either watching, or would be informed later.

"Thank you," she muttered, thinking that she didn't know enough nice people. Of course the people at her new church were nice, but she didn't know any of them that well, since she'd only been attending church for a few months.

When the clerk handed her the cone, Georgette gave it an experimental lick, confirming that Bob was right about the exotic flavor—it wasn't bad, but it was a strange combination.

On their way back to work they walked faster than she would have liked, but they didn't have time to dawdle.

"The phone hasn't stopped ringing, Bob." She paused to stifle her smile. Apparently there had been an ad in the help-wanted section of the newspaper. It had given her great pleasure to tell everyone that both positions had been filled. "Is it always like this? It hasn't been when I've shopped before."

"It never used to be this busy, but lately it has been. We hope with you here, it won't be so hectic, and we can all go home at a decent time."

She would gladly have worked as many hours as they needed, but she never would be able to explain longer hours to her father, who was not exactly pleased that she'd found a job on her own.

By the time they arrived back at the shop, both cones were finished.

"Let's get you started in the shop. Unfortunately, you'll still have run into the lobby to answer the phone, but it doesn't ring as often in the afternoon."

"Why don't you have a cordless phone?"

Bob smiled. "Sorry, but that doesn't work here. When

the phone rings, we've got power tools going or we're banging on something. It's impossible to hear the caller speak. So you really do have to leave the room."

"I didn't think of that. I understand."

"I'm going to give you all the tune-ups to do," Bob continued.

She opened her mouth to protest that she was capable of much more, but stopped herself. The terms under which she'd been hired stated light-duty. "Sure," she mumbled, trying to smile graciously.

Bob walked behind the counter and stacked a few work orders into a pile. "Do these, and when you're finished, come see me."

Georgette picked up the pile and moved the first car into Bay One, anxious to begin the job she couldn't have foreseen in her wildest dreams.

As she worked on her tune-ups and waited for the oil to drain, she watched her bosses as they worked. They both worked hard and appeared to share all tasks and decisions equally, yet they still remained friends.

Of all the people Georgette knew, she couldn't call a single woman a real friend. She seldom saw them outside formal events, and even then those events were mainly venues to make or strengthen contacts. Even at the gym, Georgette felt as if her life was a competition.

She liked to think of the guys at the track as her friends, but she never saw them anyplace else. She suspected much of that had to do with their wives and girlfriends being suspicious that she was there for more than automechanical work.

Everyone at church was friendly, but three months wasn't enough time to nurture any real friendships, especially when she only saw them once a week, and then rushed home directly after the service, since her father didn't want her going in the first place.

At four twenty-five, Bart appeared beside her. She hadn't finished the pile, but it was time to go home in five minutes.

"Didn't get as much done as you thought you would, did you?"

"No, I didn't," she said quietly.

"Before you go, Bob wants to see you. He's in the office. Okay?"

Georgette stepped out of her coveralls, hung them on the hook, picked up the pile of work orders she hadn't completed, and made her way to the lobby. Her stomach clenched with the thought that she wasn't good enough, or fast enough, and that her first day was also going to be her last.

Chapter Three

Bob paused at his customer's question, halfway through typing the invoice. "It was just a tune-up, Don," Bob responded. "I guarantee all the work we do, and I guarantee this, too." Bob hadn't hovered, but he had watched George when she couldn't tell he was there.

She knew what she was doing.

"If you tell me what you think she did wrong, I'll fix it."

"Well, maybe I spoke too quickly," his customer said. "It seems to be running smoothly, and I didn't see any oil on the ground. At least not so far."

"You won't see any, either. George did a good job."

"Do I get a discount?"

Bob gritted his teeth. "You were more than happy when my high-school-age cousin tuned up your car last year. You didn't ask for a discount then. What makes the difference now? Is it because a woman did the tune-up?"

Don's voice deepened. "No. Of course not."

Bob typed the last code for the computer to add the tax, and hit Print. "Good. Will that be on your charge card?"

A flicker of movement in the doorway to the shop caught his eye.

George was standing in the doorway, stiff as a board, holding the orders he knew she hadn't had time to do. She cleared her throat. "You wanted to see me?" she asked in a raspy squeak.

"Yes. Can you meet me in the office?"

He swiped the card, completed the transaction, closed the program, and waited until Don was out the door before he joined George. He sat behind the desk. "Bart and I had a little talk today about you."

He slid an envelope across the desk. She stiffened in the chair.

"Unfortunately, as a mechanic, you really stick out being a, um…uh…a woman. Our customers have this corporate image of us, as a business, even though there's only been the two of us. We think you'd fit in better if you didn't use those blue coveralls and bought gray ones, like ours. Bart's wife washes everything on the weekends, so buy enough to last a week. Here's a few crests with our logo. Sew them on right here." He patted the logo on his own coveralls. "Of course we'll reimburse you. This is something I should have thought of sooner. Sorry about that."

She picked up the envelope, and pulled out one of the crests. "This is what you wanted to see me about? My coveralls?" Her blue eyes, big and wide, and very, very pretty took him in.

Her voice lowered to barely above a whisper. "I thought you would be angry because I didn't finish everything you gave me."

"That's nothing to get angry about. We knew you wouldn't be able to finish everything in that pile in one day, especially with the way the phones have been ringing. But we would like you to get those coveralls as soon you can. I could probably phone the place I usually go. They size them by height. How tall are you?"

Her cheeks darkened. "I'm five foot three. I hope you're not going to ask me what I weigh."

"I have three sisters and one of my brothers is married." A smile tugged at his lips. "I know better."

"You have brother*s* and sister*s*? Plural?"

"Yes. I have three sisters and two brothers. It's a large family. What about you?"

"I only have one sister. She's married, so I don't see her much anymore."

"I don't see my family as often as I used to since I switched churches." He shrugged his shoulders. "But that's okay. I still see them at family functions and stuff."

"You can't see your family because of church? I don't understand."

"Well, every Sunday I play on my church's worship team with three of my friends. Actually, four friends, now. You remember me mentioning the accountant? His name is Adrian. He's one of them."

Her eyes widened as she stared at him in open astonishment. "My church has a lady who plays the piano, which my father tried to get me to learn as a child, but I just couldn't get it. What do you play?"

"Drums."

Her eyes flitted to his arms, before returning to his face. "I've never seen drums in church. But then I've only ever been to one."

The words were out of his mouth before he had the chance to think. "You're more than welcome to come and worship with us one Sunday. It's a very contemporary service, and the crowd is very informal. Sunday evenings we have coffee and donuts after the service."

Her eyes widened even more than they had before. "Coffee and donuts? At church?"

"Uh, yeah…" He let his voice trail off, not knowing how to reply. Her surprise told him that she hadn't been a Christian very long.

"I'd love to go. Thank you so much for inviting me. Can you write down the address?"

Warnings about not mixing business with pleasure clanged through his head. George had done well today, but today was only one day. If her skills and abilities didn't mesh with what they needed, and if he became too friendly with her, it would cloud his ability to make a rational judgment when her probationary period was over. That clashed with his duty toward her fledgling Christianity, which included widening her Christian circles. He couldn't very well take back his invitation.

He scribbled down the address for Faith Community Fellowship. "Would you like directions? It's actually not far from here."

She scooped the paper up quickly. "That's okay. I'm sure I can find it. I can hardly wait."

He pictured the way most people dressed for church, compared to the way George had been dressed when she first arrived that morning.

A newcomer was always noticed, especially during the evening service. A newcomer, coming with him, dressed to the nines, would be almost newsworthy enough to make the bulletin. He wouldn't hear the end of it for months.

"Just one thing. Like I said, it's really informal there. Please, wear jeans."

* * *

"It's Sunday night. Where are you going?"

Georgette smiled at her father. "I'm meeting a friend from work. Then we'll be having coffee and donuts. Don't wait up for me! Bye, Daddy!"

She closed the door behind her before her father could question her further. Every day, he became increasingly irritated at the lack of details she provided him about her job, but she didn't know what to tell him. Her clothes on the first day, suitable for work in an office, let him initially believe what he wanted to believe. But the questions became more and more insistent, and she'd finally told her father she was working as an assistant for two gentleman entrepreneurs in a limited partnership. She had told him her primary job was working in the accounting department, but part of her duties involved customer service.

He watched her leave daily, openly showing displeasure that she was going to work. However, at the same time, he seemed proud that she dressed well. He'd even noticed her new bright-red nail polish, and asked if it was because she was trying to attract a man.

Georgette detested wearing nail polish. She did it to hide the grease she couldn't get out from under her fingernails. She took the nail polish off on the way to work, while sitting in traffic, then put it back on, on the way home.

She knew Bob wondered why she arrived at work every day dressed to impress and then changed clothes, but she found herself caught in a cycle she couldn't break. In order to make the long drive across town and be on time, she had to leave before her father. She couldn't let him see her leaving the house wearing anything other than what his preconceived ideas told him she should be wearing.

So the household staff wouldn't have to lie for her, Georgette changed back into her good clothes in the gas station washroom on the way home. But, once at home, she changed in order to work on the old truck in the garage, so her father wouldn't wonder why she smelled like oil at supper time.

Instead of confronting her father, she was acting like a coward.

She pushed that thought aside as she pulled into the parking lot of a well-cared-for building that looked as if it had once housed some kind of small business. Inside, everything had been renovated and decorated in neutral shades of greens and browns, giving the place a welcoming atmosphere. Signs indicated that classrooms and a gymnasium were downstairs. As she stepped forward, soft music from the worship team echoed in the background.

A couple welcomed her as they gave her a bulletin.

"Welcome to Faith Community Fellowship. My name is Kaitlyn," the woman said, smiling. "Are you new to the area?"

Georgette smiled back. "No, I actually don't live near here. I'm here with Bob Delanio, except he had to come early."

The woman's eyebrows arched. She quickly glanced at the man she was with, then turned back to Georgette. "Then you'll want to go in right now, so you can find a seat close to the front. Would you like me to show you where to go?"

Georgette shook her head. "I'll just follow the music. Thanks."

As she'd said, Georgette followed the music until she was in the sanctuary where Bob, two other men and a woman were at the front.

Georgette slid into a chair, and surreptitiously she checked the place out. It was nothing like the church she'd been attending.

Even though she felt strange, she had worn jeans because Bob had told her to do so. Now she was glad she'd listened to him. Everyone was wearing either jeans or casual clothes. Not a single man wore a tie, including a man she thought might be the pastor.

Instead of a stately sanctuary with stained-glass windows and wooden benches, this sanctuary was a large rectangular room. A large opening in the wall showed a kitchen, which indicated that the sanctuary also doubled as a banquet hall. But for now, a single, plain wooden cross at the front, and banners on the walls clearly defined it as a church setting.

Most of the people in attendance were her age, except for a large group of teens, who took up at least a quarter of the seats in the back.

At the church she'd been going to, everyone was solemn, and once inside the sanctuary, silent.

Here, all around her, people talked and even laughed. Out loud.

"Hello, everyone!" a voice boomed from the speakers mounted on the walls. "Welcome to Faith Community Fellowship. Please stand and let's worship God together."

Georgette hustled to her feet. To her surprise, the first song was from one of her praise CDs that her father hadn't managed to find and throw out.

She forced herself not to watch Bob, and to pay attention to the words.

Until now, the only time she'd actually sung God's praises out loud was in the closed car, but here things were different. The enthusiasm of the crowd around her encouraged her to ignore her father's warnings not to make a spectacle of herself. Here, she joined in with the rest of the congregation to praise God in song. Being able to express herself out loud among other people opened a rush of emotion she hadn't experienced before.

By the time they had sung the fifth song in praise and wonderment of God's glory, tears streamed from her eyes, and she didn't care if her mascara ran.

When the songs were over, she quickly reached down and started digging through her purse for a tissue.

Bob sat beside her just as she was blowing her nose. "Hi, George. I'm glad you found us."

She nodded and stuffed the used tissue into her purse to hide it, taking her notepad out to record the sermon. "I've never been to a place like this." She stopped as the pastor began speaking.

Bob whispered, "If you want, we can get a tape. Randy records everything for the church's tape library."

She stopped writing. "Really? I can have one?"

"Of course."

At the end of the pastor's message, Bob rose quietly and returned to the front. The worship team closed the service with one more song, one that she knew she would hear in her head all week long, encouraging her to think about God more over the days to come.

The congregation quickly left their seats and flocked to the back of the room, where coffee and trays of do-nuts sat on a large table. Georgette was in the process of reaching for a donut when a man with dark hair and vivid blue eyes shuffled in beside her.

"You must be George, the mechanic."

Immediately, she backed up. The man grabbed a Boston cream donut, and smiled at her. "I'm Randy. Bob told us you'd be here tonight and I saw you together. You'd better grab that donut fast. The Boston creams go quickly."

Before she could think of something to say, Bob's voice sounded from behind her. "You don't waste any time, do you?"

Randy shrugged his shoulders. "If you snooze, you lose."

Bob stiffened. "I gather you've met my friend, Randy?"

She smiled. "Briefly."

As they spoke, the other members of the worship team joined them.

"Everyone, this is George, the new mechanic and bookkeeper I told you about. George, this is Paul, Celeste, and Adrian."

Adrian, the only one of the four men who wore glasses, smiled. "Welcome, we hope to see you back here."

Georgette nodded. "Yes, I think you will." She doubted she would be able to attend the morning services at Bob's church because of her obligations to her father, but she was free to attend Bob's church on Sunday evenings, especially since her father thought she was going out on a social visit, not to church.

She looked up at Bob, who was now standing beside her.

She couldn't help but like him, even though she told herself what she was feeling was simply a schoolgirl's crush, a few years too late. For the first time she was happy with her life, and everything centered around Bob.

However, it was neither practical nor wise to become personally involved with one's boss, regardless of his strength of character. She enjoyed her job too much to jeopardize it in any way.

Bob spoke up, "We have to go put our stuff away. I'll be right back."

Celeste shook her head. "I can pack up the drums for you. Why don't you two visit? We can all go out for coffee together. You're not in a rush to get home, are you, George?"

The opposite. Since her father thought she was going out to visit friends, he wouldn't expect her back for a long time. "No. That sounds like fun."

Bob's friends all returned to the front, leaving her alone with him, or as alone as they could be in the crowd.

"What did you think? You were saying this is quite different from where you're going."

"Yes. Where I've been is quite formal. Your church doesn't even have pews."

Bob nodded. "Yes. We also use this room for banquets and things like the women's auxiliary functions."

Her heart ached, thinking of just sitting around with a group of women, talking about nothing in particular—not about who was cheating on whom or the other backstabbing theatrics that passed for conversation in her current social circle.

Bob told her about how his parents and most of the rest of his family attended the main church, of which this one was a plant. While they talked, a bunch of the teens cleared and stacked the chairs to make the place ready for the next group using the room.

Just as the last of the chairs were stacked away, Randy joined them.

"Sorry, I can't go with you, after all. I have to go to Pastor Ron's place to fix his computer."

Bob nodded. "I guess I'll see you Wednesday, then." Bob turned to Georgette. "We practice at Adrian's house every Wednesday night for the coming Sunday."

She knew Bob worked every evening except Wednesday. Now she knew why. "You mean even when you're this far behind, you stop working and go do church stuff?"

"Yup. Every Wednesday."

Georgette studied Bob's face, which held nothing except honesty. Taking time off meant a loss of income. She couldn't imagine what her father would have thought of someone willingly taking a financial loss on a regular basis to do something for church. "That's pretty dedicated," she muttered.

Bob smiled. "God's done a lot for me. This is only one small thing I can do for Him. Besides, it's something I enjoy."

She could imagine that after a frustrating day, or week, there might be significant release in being able to whack a drum set.

Paul was coming down the steps of the stage as they were starting to go up. "I just remembered that I have a super early staff meeting tomorrow morning I need to prep for. I'll have to take a rain check. Sorry."

Bob blinked and looked at Paul. "Must be a very early meeting. See you Wednesday, then."

They passed Paul and got up on the stage just as Adrian closed the zipper on the electric piano case. Celeste stood off to the side, talking on her cell phone.

"Celeste's mother needs some help moving some furniture. I'm sorry, we can't go after all."

Bob's eyes narrowed. "On Sunday night? This just came up *now?*"

Adrian shrugged his shoulders. "Sorry. See you Wednesday."

Bob rested his fists on his hips as Adrian carried off the electric piano. Celeste tucked her phone into her purse, picked up Adrian's guitar case, waved, and also walked off the stage.

"If I didn't know better…" Bob muttered. He turned to Georgette. "I guess that means it's just you and me. Still want to go out for coffee and a donut?"

Georgette's foolish heart fluttered. While she'd certainly enjoyed working with him, she had also learned in casual conversation that Bob was single. Very single. Besides, she would have been stupid if she couldn't recognize the way people in the church did a double-take at seeing Bob at church with a woman.

She also had her suspicions about why Bob's friends had suddenly changed their minds about joining them for coffee.

Going out with Bob away from a work setting wasn't smart.

Georgette looked up into his eyes and cleared her throat.

"Yes."

Chapter Four

Bob unlocked the door to the lobby promptly at 7:00 am, punched in the alarm code, then headed straight for the coffee machine.

He couldn't remember the last time he'd needed coffee so badly.

At first he'd been a little nervous about going to the twenty-four-hour donut shop with George alone, but today he had no regrets. They'd talked, they'd laughed and they'd talked some more. It was well after midnight by the time they'd realized they both should have been home asleep. Bob couldn't remember the last time he'd been so tired after a weekend, but he also couldn't remember the last time he'd enjoyed himself so much.

It told him it had been too long since he'd set the worries of the business aside, and gone out to do something just because it was fun. Now that he had help in the shop, he could look forward to trying some new things.

People started coming in before the coffee was ready, dropping off their cars on the way to work.

Bart arrived as usual at seven-thirty and George arrived with enough time to run into the washroom, change and be at her station for eight o'clock.

Bob shook his head. He had no idea why she did such a thing, but he had to admit he enjoyed watching her run by before she re-emerged in the shapeless coveralls.

When the washroom door opened, Bob had her coffee poured, complete with double cream and no sugar.

"Thanks, Bob," she mumbled as she closed her eyes to take her first slow, luxurious sip, then sighed. "What's lined up for today?"

"About the same, nothing critical. We'll get the morning rush caught up, then you can get back to the bookkeeping."

"Okay." She nodded, then took a bigger sip of the hot coffee. "The way you've got me splitting my duties is working really well. I'm making good progress."

Bob smiled. He was pleased with how fast she was getting everything organized, and Adrian would be even more pleased. "Great. We've got the usual tune-ups lined up for the morning, but after lunch I've got some bigger jobs for you."

He started to go over the row of work orders pinned to the board with George when the electronic chime for the door sounded.

They both turned simultaneously as a tall, good-looking man in an expensive suit walked in.

George fumbled her coffee mug, spilling a little over the edge. A splash of coffee dribbled onto one boot.

Bob stared at this new potential customer, one better dressed than the majority of people who walked in off the street. He'd probably had a breakdown mid-trip, as the neighborhood wasn't exactly the center of the high-rise financial district.

Instead of looking at Bob, as most potential customers did when they needed help, the newcomer only had eyes…and raised eyebrows, for George. He surveyed her from head to safety-workboot covered toes.

"Hello, Georgette."

Her voice came out barely above a whisper. "Hello, Tyler."

Tyler gazed around the room, taking in everything from the work board to the coffee machine to the old couch, and treating Bob as just another furnishing. Bob tried not to take it personally.

"I need some work done on my car." Tyler focused on the crest on George's coveralls, blinked, then looked back up to her face. "Can you help me?"

George cleared her throat. "What seems to be the problem? With your car."

"It, uh… It makes this noise every once in a while, and I thought I should have it looked at."

It was Bob's gut feeling that there wasn't really anything wrong with Tyler's car, and that Tyler was there only to see George.

To give them some privacy, he walked into the shop.

"Hey, Bob, did you see what just pulled in?"

He turned toward Bart. *I don't want to know what Tyler drives,* Bob thought. "What?" he asked.

Bart jerked his head in the direction of Bay Four's open door.

He could see a shiny new Porsche through the large opening.

A Porsche so new that any alleged noise would be covered by the warranty, and could be fixed at the dealership.

Bob resolutely ignored the car, fixing his attention instead on the large window between the office and the shop. George was standing at the counter, writing something down. Tyler was leaning forward, resting his elbows on the counter.

"Looks like you've got competition," Bart's voice drifted from behind him.

Bob spun around.

"No one is competing," he mumbled, then began searching through his tool caddy for just the right wrench.

"If you say so." Bart shrugged, then turned around to continue his current project.

As soon as Bart was busy, Bob turned to watch Georgette.

She didn't seem very excited to see her acquaintance, and Bob didn't know why he found that comforting. Her behavior reinforced it—she shook her head a few times, then glanced through the window, straight at him.

Bob quickly turned his head down and continued his search for the wrench. When he found his spare, he picked it up and turned to continue the job he was supposed to be doing when the movement of the door of Tyler's Porsche opening caught his eye. Slowly and carefully, the Porsche was backed out of the parking spot and driven away, purring like the well-tuned machine it was, not a suspicious noise to be heard.

Bob pulled the rag out of his pocket, wiped his hands, and returned to the lobby, where George was busily typing purchase orders into the computer.

"I see your friend left."

He waited for her to deny that Tyler was her friend, but she didn't.

"I told him that if he thought there was a problem,

he should take it back to the dealership where he got it, because anything wrong would still be under warranty."

He again waited for her to say something more, *anything,* but silence hung between them.

He cleared his throat and stepped behind the counter. "Let's go over today's lineup together."

She nodded silently as he paged through the orders. When he'd divided up the work for the day, she logged off the computer, picked up her pile, and made her way quietly into the shop.

Bob couldn't remember the last time a day had dragged this way. Even though the three of them didn't talk any more or any less than they had in the past week, a heavy silence seemed to hang in the building, despite the constant noise of their repair work.

His earlier thoughts about shaking up his social life continued to echo through his head during the rest of the day. He was thirty years old and ready to settle down. Yet, he couldn't remember the last time he'd had a steady girlfriend.

Only days ago, Adrian and Celeste had announced to the worship team that they were getting married. That, along with Bart's endless baby pictures, reminded Bob how boring and predictable his life had become.

Of course, to start something with George would be unwise. She was his employee. However, that didn't mean they couldn't hang out as friends. Her reaction to Tyler indicated that although she had some sort of history with him, it didn't appear to be romantic.

When it was time for George to go home, she disappeared into the washroom to clean up and Bob moved to the large window in preparation. When the washroom door opened again and she'd cleared it by a few steps,

Bob entered the lobby, hoping she would think the timing was coincidental.

George started in surprise at seeing him in the lobby at that hour of the day, without the phone ringing. "Goodnight, Bob," she said on her way to the door. "See you tomorrow."

"Wait," he said, and she stopped.

"Before you go, I wanted to ask you something. I haven't been able to go as often as I used to, but every Monday night my church has a Bible study. It's at the home of one of the deacon couples, and it's really informal. I was wondering if you'd like to go with me tonight."

She blinked a few times, then glanced toward the door. "Sorry, I can't," she mumbled, then kept walking. She opened the door, stepped outside, then just before the door closed, she said, "I'm going out with Tyler."

Georgette stepped back to look at herself in the mirror.

The housekeeper had helped to style her hair into perfect order.

It was stiff and felt artificial.

Her makeup was flawless, her shadow just the right color to accent her eyes. Her nail polish matched her lipstick. The artifice brought back a memory of posing for promotional photographs meant to encourage people to help the starving children of the world. It had raised only marginal funding, but it brought phenomenal publicity for her father. The experience was a good reminder of how shallow people could be.

Just like at that session, her outfit was the height of fashion, and emphasized her figure to perfection while binding it uncomfortably.

Her shoes were darling, and the perfect accent to her legs. They also pinched her toes, and she didn't know if she could stand more than twenty minutes in them. If she took them off under the table to wiggle her toes, she knew she would never get them back on.

Georgette looked perfect.

She felt like a fake.

"Georgie-Pie, honey, you look magnificent!"

Georgette inhaled deeply, pasted on a smile that was as phony as the rest of her appearance, and turned to face her father, who was standing in her bedroom doorway. "Thank you, Daddy. Tyler should be here in a few minutes, and I want to be ready."

"Always a stickler for punctuality." He grinned and playfully wagged one finger in the air at her. "It wouldn't hurt to be fashionably late."

"We have reservations for dinner." Besides, Georgette considered being fashionably late incredibly rude and self-centered. It was only one of many ways to draw attention to oneself. She hated that, too. "Now, if you'll excuse me, I need a few more minutes to finish getting ready." She didn't bother to watch him leave.

It was at times like this she thought of her mother, and wondered if the endless social charade was one of the things that had driven her mother away. Georgette had been very young when her mother had left. Her father had told her it was because her mother didn't want to be part of their family anymore. It had hurt terribly at the time, and still did. As an adult, though, Georgette could see how her father's tyranny made her family dysfunctional. She could only guess at the difficulty of being married to him. She often thought about how bad it must have been to make her mother run away and abandon her two children.

On the way to the closet, Georgette's step faltered. She had one picture of her mother left that her father hadn't found and destroyed. She kept it hidden in the lining of her purse, and whenever she switched purses, she made sure the picture went with her. It would never do to have her father find it now. She turned in time to see her father close the door behind him.

When the door was closed, Georgette dumped the contents of her purse haphazardly onto the bed, but she carefully removed the laminated and carefully preserved picture from where she'd hidden it in the seam of the lining.

She paused to sit on the bed to study the picture, and to remember.

As an adult, the resemblance between her and her mother was strong. They had the same light-blond hair color, the same blue eyes, and, sadly, the same lack of height. The picture had been taken only days before her mother had left. Georgette had been ten years old, and the two of them had been together, laughing and making rabbit ears behind each other's heads with their fingers.

Josephine had taken the picture in the afternoon, while her father was at work. He never would have permitted such nonsense if he'd been there. Georgette had sneaked the picture out of the package and taken it to school to show a friend. When she'd arrived back home, not only was her mother gone, but so was everything her mother owned, and every reminder of her. It was a clean sweep. All she had left of her mother was one candid photograph and a small gold cross on a delicate gold chain that she never took off, not even at night.

"Georgie-Pie, honey. He's here!"

She gently tucked the photograph into its new secret

hiding spot in the new purse lining, then rammed everything else in as quickly as she could. "I'll be right there!" she called, taking one last look at herself in the mirror. She stuck out her tongue at her reflection, stiffened and walked slowly, in a dignified manner, out of the bedroom, and down the stairs.

Tyler smiled, but he didn't leave her father's side. "You look lovely, Georgette."

"Thank you, Tyler," she said gracefully. She batted her eyelashes coyly, positive that Tyler wouldn't catch her sarcasm.

Bob would have caught it if she did such a thing to him. In fact, Bob would have laughed.

She should have been with Bob right now. She'd been thrilled that he'd invited her to a Bible study meeting. But instead, she was with Tyler because she couldn't take the chance he would tell her father he'd seen her. She needed to talk to Tyler immediately.

Tyler held the car door open for her and whisked her away to an intimate and very expensive restaurant.

She was almost surprised he hadn't taken her somewhere splashy, somewhere people they knew would see them, but she guessed Tyler wanted the privacy rather than the notoriety, at least for the moment.

They made polite chitchat until their meals came and the waiter made the obligatory last visit to make sure everything was satisfactory before leaving them alone.

Georgette had been dreading the moment they would be assured of privacy.

"So, tell me, Georgette, what in the world were you doing at that place?"

"I think it should be obvious. I work there. What were *you* doing there?" She still didn't know if she'd ever overcome the shock of seeing someone she knew on that side of town.

"I told you what I was doing there. I was on my way downtown when I heard a noise. I must have just run over something, because the noise didn't happen again."

Georgette poked at her salmon with her fork. "I suppose," she said. It was possible, but unlikely. Bob And Bart's was nowhere near the route between Tyler's home and his office downtown. The only way Tyler, or anyone, for that matter, would have run into her was if they already knew she was there, because it wasn't the type of neighborhood any of her acquaintances would normally ever go to.

She cleared her throat. "I meant, what were you doing there in the first place? It's kind of out of your way, isn't it?"

Tyler flashed her his most charming smile—a smile clearly meant to distract her from their conversation. "It might be a little out of my way, but I felt like taking an indirect route that day."

Indirect, nothing. His little side trip doubled his commute.

Unless he had been following her...

"Was there any particular reason you felt like going out of your way? Did you see my car when I was on the way to work or anything?"

"Yes, actually, I did see your car. That's why I stopped in. When I walked in the door, I was certainly surprised to see you. And what a getup!"

She noted that he avoided any mention of when he'd seen her car. She was positive it wasn't in the parking lot. It was long before that. A long, long time before that. Possibly when she was backing out of the garage at home. He could have been behind her the whole time, following her, and she wouldn't have noticed. Of course, if she accused him of following her, he would never admit it.

She narrowed her eyes. "Lots of people wear uniforms and the like, you know."

Tyler choked on his mouthful, swallowed, coughed and cleared his throat. "But not like that. I could see you doing accounting, but why are you delivering parts?"

Georgette's heart skipped a beat. She wasn't ready for anyone she knew, especially someone so close to her father, to know what she was doing. But she'd been caught and now it was time to defend her choices.

"I don't deliver parts. I work in the shop, fixing things. Getting my hands dirty." Georgette laid her knife and fork down, and clasped those hands in front of her. "And that's exactly the job I wanted. I'm only doing the accounting because I couldn't get one without the other."

Tyler shook his head. "You should be working for your father."

Been there, done that. She hated her father manipulating her like a puppet on a string. This was her first chance at independence, and nothing was going to take it away from her. Nothing. "Maybe. But for now, this is what I want to do."

"What could that two-bit outfit possibly be paying you to make it worth your while?"

Georgette sighed. She wasn't there for the money. The allowance her father gave her for the hour a day she spent managing his charities was more than double her full-time salary. It was one more thing her father used to control her, paying her for her loyalty. It made her feel as if she was being bought, and she hated herself for it.

"Auto mechanics is a hobby for me, so I consider this a hobby that pays."

"You know what your father would say if he found out, don't you?"

She shuddered at the thought. He would consider what she was doing pure defiance, and in a way, it was. But it was also the only place where she was out from under her father's thumb. Even though she'd told Tyler she considered it a hobby, she worked hard at her job and when the day was done, she was at peace with herself and with God, and she could sleep well at night.

She raised one hand up, pressing into the tiny cross, something else her father didn't approve of. "I don't think I'm ready to tell Daddy the specifics yet." In fact, she didn't know if she would ever be ready to tell him. But at the same time, she knew that one day she would have to. To think otherwise was unrealistic.

"Tell me, Georgette, does anyone else know? Besides me?"

Her breath caught in her throat. "I don't know," she muttered, at least she hoped and prayed no one knew. That Tyler knew was not in her favor.

He leaned forward toward her, over the table. "I could help you keep your secret."

Her heart began to pound. She didn't trust Tyler, but he had her between a rock and a hard place. Perhaps graciousness on her part would evoke a similar response. "Could you? I'd really appreciate that." She wondered nervously what he would ask for in return. She had nothing to offer. To offer money would be an insult. Any work he would ever need done to his car was best done by the dealership where he bought it.

"But in return, there's something you can do for me."

Here it was. She leaned closer to Tyler. "What do you have in mind?"

Tyler sat back and crossed his arms over his chest. "I need to attend a number of functions, and it doesn't look good for me to go alone. I need you there as my companion. Your father would be pleased to see us together, you know, in the past, he's encouraged me to spend time with you."

Georgette forced herself to breathe. Tyler came from old money, but that wasn't enough for Tyler. He was ambitious, which shouldn't have been bad, except that like her father, Tyler didn't care who he stepped on.

"I don't know…" she let her voice trail off, trying to give herself more time to think.

Tyler tipped his head to one side. "You scratch my back, I'll scratch yours."

Maybe to him, it was back-scratching. To Georgette, it sounded an awful lot like extortion.

But until she could figure out a way to approach her father, she didn't have any choice. By not dealing with the problem sooner, she had set herself up to become an easy victim.

"I can't believe that you, of all people, would be unable to find a date. I'm sure there are any number of women who want to go out with you."

"Maybe. But it looks better if I go to these things with the same person. It gives me a reputation for stability and maturity."

Georgette's blood boiled. What Tyler looked like on

the outside to strangers was more important to him than anything.

Bob would never have behaved in such a manner. Even though Bob wasn't in the upper echelons of the corporate world, he was still a successful business owner. He was a good Christian man, and he made an income he was comfortable with. His entire business was built on one thing. Doing honest work in order to satisfy his customers.

The only one Tyler wanted to satisfy was himself, no matter what the cost.

"How many times? Does today count?"

"Today we're negotiating. Does this mean you agree?"

For now, Georgette didn't have a choice. Soon she would find an appropriate time to tell her father, on her own terms, but until the time was right, she would have to put up with Tyler.

"I agree," she muttered, then pushed the plate containing her half-eaten meal slightly forward on the tabletop. "Do you mind if we leave? I'm not as hungry as I thought I was."

Tyler signaled the waiter for the bill, but continued eating. "Great. Today is Monday. I've got to go to a wild-life fund-raiser on Wednesday. I'll pick you up at five-thirty. It's a dinner engagement. Dress appropriately."

Chapter Five

Georgette pushed a little more sawdust over the spill with the toe of her workboot. "It should be absorbed by tomorrow," she mumbled to Bart, who reached out to run his finger along the seal of the leaky oil filter of the car on the hoist above them.

Bob appeared beside her. "Did you find out what's wrong?"

Georgette nodded. "I don't know where she went to change the oil, and I don't know how they could have done it, but the O-ring was twisted and it wrecked the seal. That's what's been causing the leak."

Bart looked up and watched as another drop leaked out. "Mrs. Jablonski is going to be happy. She was so afraid of what it would cost to fix, she's just been adding more oil instead of bringing it in. The only reason she finally came was because her neighbors were complaining about the growing puddle on the street." All we have to charge her for is changing the filter."

"You mean you're not even going to charge her for the full oil-change package?" Her father's mechanic charged a service fee just to look at any vehicle, then took the money off the cost of the repair later. However, if nothing was done, they kept the money for their time, which was only fair.

"Naw. It took under a minute to see what the problem was. Besides, we never charge for estimates."

"But how are you going to make money on this, then?"

"Mrs. Jablonski is living on a pension. We'll get back our time in the markup on the new filter we're going to give her, so it's not like we're losing anything. The only reason she brought it here is because my mother told her I would look at it and fix it for a fair price. I'm not doing it for free. I'm just being reasonable."

"But…" She let her voice trail off. An oil filter wasn't free, but it was still an inexpensive item. She couldn't imagine there was much markup on it. It might pay for one minute worth of their time, when calculating all the expenses that went with running a business. Georgette turned to Bart. "And you agree with this decision?"

Bart shrugged his shoulders. "I don't do anything to contradict a promise made by Bob's mama. This, you too, will learn." He turned to Bob. "Don't forget to give Mrs. Jablonski the seniors' discount."

In response, Bob nodded.

All Georgette could do was stare.

Her father had always drilled into her head to get top dollar, no matter what. Charity work, when plainly labeled *charity,* was different. Her father received his rewards in publicity, product placement and good will. But in business, her father refused to open any doors where people might take advantage, and that meant no favors. The point of being in business wasn't merely to survive. He risked money to make money, and he protected his investments. The first thing her father had taught her was that nice guys always finished last.

Georgette looked around her. The building that housed the auto repair shop was old—showing both wear and age. The lobby and the washrooms had been renovated at least once, and the walls needed another couple of coats of paint. And that was just for starters. For their modest requirements, the building was adequate, but not much more.

She couldn't see that either Bart or Bob were doing much better personally.

Bart had just purchased a new vehicle, but it was only a mid-priced minivan. Yet, he was proud of his family-man vehicle. Bob's car was also mid-priced, mid-sized and three years old, a year older than any car her father ever owned. For two men who were risking everything they had to keep their business going, they weren't very far ahead.

Because they were nice guys.

But as far as she could tell, even though Bob worked hard, he was happy. And Georgette was happy working for him.

That was why she was taking the risk she was now taking, and why she had accepted Tyler's terms for his silence in keeping her secret from her father. For the first time in her life, she was happy. She was doing something she wanted to do, dealing with people who had nothing to gain by knowing her.

Besides, it didn't seem like her father's world held anything Bob would want. He was conscientious and honest, and lived his life the way God wanted him to. The more she came to know Bob as she worked with him, the more she liked him both personally and professionally. She couldn't say the same about Tyler.

Georgette sighed. For now, she was simply *George the Mechanic*. But tonight, she would again have to become *Georgette the Fake* to help Tyler rub elbows to further himself and his business ventures. She'd much rather help Bob with his business ventures, but he didn't need a pretty showpiece. He needed a good mechanic and a proficient bookkeeper, not to mention some extra money for renovations.

She had the money, but she couldn't give it to him without revealing her background. She also knew he'd find the gift insulting. For now, all she could do to help him was be the best mechanic and best employee she could be.

"I should be finished this in twenty minutes. What have you got for me next?"

"Every large job we have right now is waiting for parts. I've got the orders lined up on the board. Just take the next up, Bart and I will do the same, and by tomorrow we should be all caught up and ready for when the backlog of parts comes in."

She kept busy all day, but when the day was done, she felt satisfied about her contribution.

She unzipped her coveralls, stepped out of them, made a quick inspection to see if they were still acceptable for one more day without a trip through the washing machine, then hung them on the hook at her station.

As she squatted and reached into the bottom of her tool caddy to retrieve her purse, footsteps echoed on the concrete floor behind her. She turned to see Bob towering above her.

"I'm sorry I didn't catch you sooner. I was wondering if you wouldn't mind staying an hour later tonight to finish up the last order on the board. Tonight is

Wednesday, practice night for the worship team. I've got be out of here at six-thirty, and I had really wanted to get everything done so we'll be ready for tomorrow morning. I'll pay you overtime. I don't expect you to do it for nothing."

Georgette's heart sank. "I'm so sorry. Any other day, I'd love to stay. But tonight I have to be somewhere at five-thirty, and I can't." She checked her watch. It was four-thirty on the dot, and even leaving on time, she was pressing her luck. By the time she made the trip across town in rush-hour traffic, including her quick change back into her skirt and blouse in the washroom at the gas station, which left only fifteen minutes to shower, wash, dry her hair and run the curling iron through it, and scramble into the dress, hose and accessories that she'd already set aside.

"Oh. Sorry. Don't worry about it. I'll just come back after the practice is over and finish up."

"You'd do that?"

"They just called and said they needed the car tomorrow morning, so I said I would do it. I try not to make promises I can't keep."

Georgette stepped closer, "You put in such long hours. I know you're often here at six-thirty in the morning to take people's cars in before they go to work when you're not scheduled to be in until seven." Frequently he even stayed very late to get a job done, which it appeared would happen again tonight. "How about if I come in early tomorrow?"

Bob shook his head. "No. You're going on a date tonight, and I don't want you to ruin your evening by cutting your night short so you can come in early."

Georgette bit back a smile. Needing to go home early

would work in her favor. "I really didn't plan to be out late, anyway. I'm sure Tyler will understand."

He stiffened. "Tyler seems very understanding. I know a lot of guys who wouldn't want their wives or girlfriends doing a job like this."

Not to mention daughters. Her father immediately came to mind, as both an understatement and a confirmation of Bob's statement.

She looked up at Bob. "Actually, I really hate going out to the kind of places Tyler and I are going tonight. It's a big animal shelter fund-raiser and even though I know it's a worthy cause, I'd still rather just make a donation than get all dressed up and go to a banquet with people I don't care about seeing. They're only there to see who's currently with whom, and to try to make an impression. Even if we didn't have this project at work, I have something in my garage at home I'd be doing. It's something I've been working on for a long time." Strangely, she found that her new job hadn't lessened her joy in fixing up the old pickup truck. If she kept it up, the old beast would be running very soon.

Bob smiled, and his eyes became unfocused. "Yeah. I have a project like that." He smiled and looked off into the distance for a few seconds. Suddenly, he recollected himself. "I'm keeping you. You're going to be late."

Once again, she checked her watch. It was getting later by the minute, yet she wasn't motivated to hurry. "I guess," she replied.

"I'll take you up on that offer another day. Goodnight, George."

She nodded. "Sure. Goodnight, Bob."

Randy Reynolds did the same thing he always did at the end of a good practice. He headed right into Adrian's kitchen, grabbed first choice of the donuts, poured a fresh cup of coffee, then sauntered back into Adrian's den while everyone tidied up their music and put their instruments away.

"Hey, Randy, you could always help, you know," Bob called out.

Randy turned toward his best friend, took a bite out of the donut, then waved it at Bob as he spoke. "You're only saying that because taking down the drum set takes the longest."

"Which means you should help me every week instead of stuffing your face."

Randy pressed his hand onto his stomach, being careful not to smear any of the icing from the donut onto his shirt. "I'm a growing boy."

Celeste shook her head while she wound up one of the patch cords. "I don't know how you stay so slim; you eat so much junk food."

Randy grinned. "It's a gift. Besides, this might be my only chance to get my favorite donuts for a whole week, at least for free. Did you see Bob's new girlfriend at church Sunday night? She likes the same kind of donuts I do."

"She's not my girlfriend," Bob muttered as he started disassembling the stool. "She's my new light-duty mechanic."

Randy snorted. "And that's why you took her to church? My boss never takes me to church."

"That's different."

"Yeah, right."

"It's true. She's my employee. She works for me and that's all."

Randy tried not to laugh, but failed. "Methinks thou doth protest too much," he chortled.

Bob sighed as he tucked the seat into the case. "I'm not protesting. I'm stating a fact. Besides, she's got a boyfriend, and tonight he's taking her to a fund-raising banquet downtown."

Randy froze. "Don't you think that's a little strange?"

"No. Lots of people go to those kind of things. It's how they raise money for worthy causes."

Randy noticed that both Adrian and Paul had suddenly become silent, and were watching his conversation with Bob. So they wouldn't listen in, Randy shoveled the rest of the donut into his mouth, set his coffee mug on Paul's amp, and shuffled in closer to Bob.

"When I asked if you thought it was strange that she was going to something like that, I didn't mean that it's a bad thing to give money to help the animals. I meant, it's not your average mechanic-type person who goes to things like that. I saw mention of that event in the community pages in the paper, and it's pretty pricey. When's the last time you went to a fund-raising banquet like that?"

Bob opened his mouth to reply, but Randy quickly raised one hand to silence him.

"You don't have to tell me. I know the answer. The answer is never. When you make a donation, you just make a donation. Not only that, but those things usually run hundreds of dollars a plate. I'm not saying that it's not a good thing to do, but you see a lot of people who are there for the same reason as the Pharisee on the street showing how wonderful he was to everyone who cared to look."

Bob's eyebrows knotted.

"What?" Randy asked.

"Funny you should say that. George said something very similar, only she didn't spell it out quite like you did. She's only going because her boyfriend wants to go."

Randy whistled between his teeth. "Your low-paid new mechanic must have a very rich boyfriend to go to stuff like that."

Bob squirmed. "She's not that low-paid. I'm paying her what we can afford, until we see if this works out. It's also an entry-level position."

"I think you know what I meant."

Bob's voice dropped to a gravelly mumble. "Who she goes out with is not my concern."

Randy moved even closer and lowered the volume of his voice even more. "Are you sure about this boyfriend? I saw the way she looked at you Sunday night. She likes you."

Bob stiffened. "She looks up to me as her boss and as someone who shares her love of mechanics. I have to admit it's kind of flattering, but that's it. You're taking it wrong."

"I don't know. I think—"

Paul's voice boomed behind him. "Will you two quit whispering and get finished? Randy, you're parked behind me in the driveway. I want to go home sometime tonight."

Randy stood. "Sorry." He tucked the pieces of the stand into the case, and turned around. "I'll be right back," he said to Bob. "Don't go away."

Randy followed Paul outside, and put his hand on the door of Paul's car, preventing Paul from opening it. "Before you leave, I want to talk to you about last Sunday night."

Paul turned around. "Sunday night? You mean when

Bob brought that girl to church? He said she was his new mechanic."

Randy nodded. "That's right. Did you see the way she was looking at him? He's not exactly a hermit, but when was the last time Bob had a steady girlfriend?"

Paul smirked. "More recently than you."

"You know what I mean. What do you think?"

Paul shrugged his shoulders. "I think you should mind your own business and leave Bob alone."

"I just found out that she's got a rich boyfriend," Randy continued. "But I saw how she looked at Bob Sunday night. Trouble's brewing especially if she tries to hook Bob. Bob won't spend his money foolishly, not on some spoiled princess. It'll break his heart when she dumps him."

"Dumps him? Princess? She's a mechanic! They're not even going out! You are insane!" Paul rolled his eyes. "Bob can handle himself just fine. And speaking of Bob, there he is." Paul raised one hand and waved at Bob, who was walking toward his car, which was parked on the street.

Randy turned around. "Hey! Where are you going? I thought we were going to talk."

Bob opened his car door. "Sorry. I don't have time. I've got to get back to work. I promised a customer I'd have his car ready by tomorrow morning, and that transmission isn't fixing itself while I'm here talking."

"Work?" Randy checked his watch. "At this hour? I thought after you hired someone, you would be cutting back your own hours."

"That day will come, but not yet. We were further behind than we thought. I hate to think of the shape we'd be in if it wasn't for George." He smiled, and his eyes became unfocused for a few seconds. He blinked, shook his head, and opened the car door. "See you on the weekend, I guess."

Before Randy could respond, the door closed, Bob started the engine, and drove off.

He turned back to Paul. "See?"

"I don't see anything except that Bob's working too much, as usual. Which means he doesn't have time for a girlfriend, even if she is right under his nose all day. Now if you'll please move your car, I have to go, too."

Chapter Six

"George? What are you doing here?" Bob clearly had not expected company at the shop.

"I wasn't having a very good time at the banquet, so I left early. Need some help?" Georgette tried to appear casual, but her stomach was completely tied up in knots. All during the banquet, all she could think of was Bob. As soon as she could, she made an excuse to leave, although she knew he could do the work himself.

"Well…" Bob's voice trailed off, and he ran his fingers through his hair. "Now that you're here, I could use a hand. But only if you're sure. You work a forty-hour week, and I don't want you to think you need to do more."

Georgette looked down at her feet, still in her best shoes. "I'm not here to put in overtime. I'm here because I'd prefer to help you with the transmission than sit at the banquet and smile for strangers."

Bob shook his head. "Fine. Two people will make the job go faster. To tell the truth, it's not so bad working such long hours when it's daylight. But when it's dark and everything outside is quiet, it feels worse because it's obvious the rest of the world is at home with their families, and I'm working late again. Once you're caught up with the bookkeeping, you'll be spending more time in the shop, and when that happens, I think we'll be able to keep up with what comes in on a daily basis without anyone having to put in much extra time."

"If it helps, I can see a difference already, even in the short time I've been working here."

"You're right about that." Bob smiled, and Georgette's heart rate suddenly accelerated.

Since the first day she'd seen Bob she'd thought he was good-looking, and the faint crow's feet which appeared at the corners of his eyes when he smiled made him more attractive. Now that she was starting to get to know him, she knew those little lines weren't from age; they were because of the kind heart behind his easy smiles.

She adjusted the strap on the duffle bag on her shoulder. "You should know I'm here on my own time; you don't have to pay me overtime."

"But—"

Georgette held up one palm to silence him. Bob needed the money far more than she did. "I mean it. If you insist on paying me overtime for this, I'm going to go back home." Not that she wanted to go home. If she did, she would have to explain to her father why she wasn't at the banquet with Tyler.

Bob sighed. "This isn't normally something I would allow, but you're not giving me a choice. Okay. On your own time. Thanks."

Just as she did every morning, Georgette hurried into the washroom to slip on her jeans and a T-shirt, then pulled her coveralls off the hook and stepped into them.

Bob had already removed the transmission and was starting to replace the first clutch plate, which was burnt.

"So you and Tyler weren't having a good time at the banquet?" he muttered as he yanked out the old piece.

Georgette leaned to the side to check the alignment on the rest. "Tyler was doing fine, but he likes those kind of things. After a while I couldn't take it anymore."

"Was Tyler okay with you leaving the banquet?"

Georgette eased up on her motions, thinking of Tyler's comments.

He hadn't been pleased, but she'd reminded him that she had fulfilled her obligations for the night, and she'd been a part of the appropriate conversations. Tyler begrudgingly conceded and took her home. Fortunately her father wasn't home yet, and Josephine was too busy vacuuming to notice her. She'd quickly grabbed her duffel and hurried out to her car, which she'd left parked on the street, and had driven away before anyone noticed that she'd been home at all.

During the drive to Bob's shop, she'd experienced a feeling of freedom such as she'd never felt before. The only thing that could have made it better was if she had been riding on a big, noisy motorcycle, the wind blowing through her hair. Still, despite her silly fantasy, she *was* free, at least for the balance of the evening.

"Tyler wasn't happy, but I didn't care. I did what I had to do."

Bob laid his wrench down on the bench. "Pardon me?"

"I only went with Tyler because I owed him a favor." The trouble was, what Tyler called a favor was better known as blackmail. Tyler had her trapped, and they both knew it.

Bob's brow knotted. "I don't understand. When I

take a date somewhere, it's somewhere we both want to go. I wouldn't enjoy myself if I knew my date didn't want to be there."

While Georgette couldn't divulge the details of her personal life, she needed Bob to think she had better sense than to go out with the likes of Tyler. She took a deep breath.

"I'm not actually dating him. He just needs to have someone with him when he goes to certain functions, and he's calling in a favor to have me go with him." Every minute she spent with Tyler made her pray even more that she could find a painless way to tell her father the nature of the job she went to every day.

"Oh…" Bob's voice trailed off. He quickly picked up the torque wrench and began tightening one of the belts on the transmission. He didn't look at her as he spoke. "I probably shouldn't stick my nose where it doesn't belong, but it sounds like you only went under protest. Please take care of yourself—you wouldn't want to end up compromising your faith."

Georgette stiffened. So far, Tyler hadn't asked her to do anything that wasn't proper, but she really didn't know how far he would push things. She knew she shouldn't have been trying to cover up her new life, but she was trapped by circumstances beyond her control.

She smiled weakly at Bob. "It's okay. I'm fine."

"Good. Let's get this back where it belongs, and we'll be done"

Bob resealed the casing, and together, they carried it back to the car and fastened it in place. He started the engine, and they watched to make sure there were no leaks.

While they waited, Bob pulled the rag out of his pocket, and wiped his hands. "I think everything's finished." He pushed at his sleeve and checked his watch. "We made good time, between the two of us. I know it's not exactly early, but can I take you out for coffee or something? Especially if you won't accept any pay for doing this."

Georgette felt a tremor of excitement. "Not tonight. I really should go home. It's getting late." Her father knew what time the banquet ended, and he would be expecting her back. "But if you'll take a rain check, I accept."

Bob smiled back, and those adorable crinkles appeared again at the corners of his beautiful green eyes. "A rain check it is, then."

She felt like skipping out of the building after she'd changed back into her finery, but she forced herself to maintain her dignity.

When she arrived at home her father was in the living room, waiting for her.

"Hi, Daddy. I'm back."

He smiled politely. "I see that. Did you have a good time?"

She shrugged her shoulders. It wouldn't do to say something bad.

"I noticed that you had your car. I thought Tyler came earlier to pick you up."

She held up the bag with the gas station's logo. Every time she used their washroom to change, she bought something as an excuse to go inside. "I had to go to the gas station."

Her father's expression tightened. "You didn't buy oil for the car, again, did you? We can have a mechanic do that. Or is this something for that ridiculous project of yours in the garage?"

"It's a snack, Daddy."

His eyes narrowed. "I hope you're watching your figure. You've been eating a lot of snacks lately."

"It's okay, Daddy. I've been exercising. I've actually lost weight in the last week."

Immediately, he softened. "That's my girl. This job must be good for you to start thinking of such things."

She couldn't help but smile back. "Yes, Daddy, this job has been very good for me. Now if you don't mind, I've had a long and busy day, and I'm tired. I'm going to bed."

Bob stopped what he was doing once again to watch George run from her car to the washroom in order to change. Every day for three months, she'd done the same thing. He could only assume that she had another part-time job, although it would have to be a very early job. He didn't like to think she needed a second job, after all, he was paying her a fair salary, considering her experience and duties.

It was none of his business, though, so today, as on every other day, Bob remained silent when the washroom door opened. George re-emerged wearing jeans, a T-shirt and the required steel-toed safety footwear.

"Hi, Bob!" she called out as she waved, then tucked her duffel under the counter, and logged in to the computer.

He waved back, then quickly turned around and resumed his task.

George was his employee, and nothing more. Yet, at the same time, he didn't want to see her working herself to death. She worked hard for him, and she did a good job. A couple of regular customers had specifically asked for her to do the work on their cars.

Not long after she'd shown up to help him on the

blown transmission that evening, he'd taken her out for dinner as a thank-you. They had had so much fun that night that they'd agreed to make dinner on Thursday evenings a standard routine. Even so, he still didn't know much about what she did away from work, and he still didn't know why she arrived every morning looking as if she was coming from another job.

Georgette Ecklington was both an asset and a mystery. He couldn't help but like her. She was feisty, spoke her mind, and wasn't afraid to get dirty. He was glad that she joined him at Faith Community Fellowship for their evening service every week. Her enthusiasm and honest questions as a new Christian were both refreshing and a reminder that he wasn't setting aside enough time for God in his own life.

As soon as they got more caught up and didn't have to work so much, that would change, and it was because of George.

"Hey, Bob! What are you doing?" Bart's voice echoed from behind him. "Why are you staring at the wall?"

"What?" Bob felt his face heat up. "Never mind," he mumbled. "I was just thinking about something."

"Yeah. Thinking about George."

Bob turned around, about to contradict his friend, but the second he opened his mouth, Bart started laughing.

"Give it up, Bob. Nothing you say can change the truth. I can tell. You've got George on the brain."

Bob gritted his teeth and tromped back to the car he was working on. *"Ma fatti affari tuoi,"* he muttered.

Bart laughed louder. "Have I touched a nerve, Roberto?" he asked, rolling his *R*s as he spoke, just as Bob's Italian-born mother did, because Bart knew it annoyed him. "Would you like to repeat that? In English?"

Bob spun around. "I said, I wish you would mind your own business."

Bart chuckled again. "I hope I haven't pushed my luck, but speaking of business, I need a favor."

"What?" Bob snapped as he crossed his arms over his chest.

"I can't go to the Chamber of Commerce dinner. Anna didn't realize it was tonight, and she bought tickets for a play. She got dinner reservations, a babysitter and everything. Can you go for me?"

Bob tapped the socket wrench repeatedly into his palm as he contemplated Bart's request. It was part of their agreement as partners that Bart would attend the few social functions related to their business, and Bob would meet with their suppliers. Occasionally they reversed the roles, but it hadn't taken long to see that Bart did better in group situations, and Bob did better working one-on-one.

But he couldn't turn down his friend's request.

"Yeah. I can go for you."

One corner of Bart's mouth turned up. "Actually, I was thinking…. Why don't you ask George? You know you hate handling this stuff alone."

Bob glanced at George, who was haggling with a customer over the price of an overhaul. She was good with people, of that there was no doubt. Bob thought he would enjoy going to the Chamber banquet with George, those Thursday-evening dinners were fun and a chance to talk about what was happening at work. It may have been a bit odd, but they both found they needed—and wanted—the break from the shop.

But there were times they didn't talk strictly business, and it was those times that gave Bob pause about asking her to accompany him. Every time Tyler took her to another "event," she spent a large part of the next Thursday evening complaining bitterly to Bob, both about Tyler and about the evenings. She always thanked Bob profusely for letting her vent her frustration, making him feel as if he'd been at least helpful.

It would have been nice not to go to the Chamber banquet by himself, but Bob knew George didn't enjoy such things.

He turned back to Bart. "It's okay. It's only a couple of hours. I'll go alone."

Chapter Seven

Georgette walked into the boutique with the bag containing her father's latest purchase tucked under her arm. She sucked in a deep breath and made her way to the counter.

"I'd like to exchange this dress," she said to the clerk, who frowned making it very clear that the store didn't approve of returns.

"Of course. What seems to be the problem?"

"I really don't like it. I want to exchange it for something more suitable. I need something classic and more understated." In other words, Georgette wanted something that would help her fade into the woodwork.

The clerk pulled the dress out of the bag. Her frown deepened. "This is odd. A gentleman bought this dress yesterday…" her voice trailed off. "Wait. William Ecklington bought this. You must be Georgette." She extended one hand. "It's a pleasure to meet you finally."

Georgette smiled politely. They had met once before, but in the shadow of her father, the woman had barely acknowledged her presence. "It's a pleasure to meet you, too. I have no idea how much my father paid for this dress, so please show me which things would constitute a straight exchange."

The woman directed her to an alcove at the back of the store, bearing a sign reading Designer Fashions, New Arrivals. Georgette couldn't see any prices from where she stood, but the security guard lurking at the entrance to the alcove made it obvious they were the most expensive in the store.

"Anything from this area can be a straight exchange."

She quickly sorted through the racks, and selected a dark-green sheath with no adornments other than a single black button at the throat. It was a simple dress, but she didn't care how she looked in it. She wanted it only for the color.

The dress was the same green as Bob's eyes.

"I'll take this one."

"Don't you want to try it on?"

That's not necessary, I love it and I know it will fit."

The woman entered the exchange in the computer, put Georgette's selection in a bag and wished her a pleasant evening.

"Thank you," Georgette said as she turned around and returned to her car. She doubted she would have a pleasant evening. Not only was she again forced to spend another evening with Tyler, but her father would also be there.

Bob straightened his tie, and walked into the banquet hall. He hated formal functions, but today's dinner was a buffet rather than sit-down meal, which allowed the guests to mingle more freely. It also meant he could leave early.

He chatted with a few people he knew, as he filled his plate, when a face he hadn't expected to see caught his attention.

Almost as if she felt his eyes on her, George turned around. The second they made eye contact, her mouth opened slightly in visible surprise. She spoke to a man to her right and left the group of people to join Bob.

Bob smiled at the sight of her. Normally, George dressed well, at least first thing in the morning. But tonight, she was positively striking.

"Hey, George. Nice dress," he said softly, meaning only to compliment, and not to make it look as though he was ogling her. "That color really suits you."

A slight blush highlighted her cheeks. "Thanks." Her voice lowered. "What are you doing here?"

Bob glanced at the group she'd just left, recognizing Tyler. "Bart couldn't make it, so I agreed to come for him. Are you enjoying yourself?"

She looked down at her plate, picked up a canapé, popped it into her mouth and grinned. "I didn't think I would have a good time, but I discovered a trick. I can put a polite amount of food on my plate, eat it all, then go back for seconds. I just have to make sure I join up with a different group of people each time, which isn't hard with a crowd like this." She pointed to her plate. "This is my fifth round of 'seconds.' Not bad, don't you think?"

His smile dropped. "So you're here with Tyler?"

"Uh…yes." She turned and searched the room, then quickly turned back to him. "But my father is here, too. My father knows Tyler's family quite well."

Part of him wanted to ask her to introduce him to her father, but part him wanted to run and hide, even though he knew the impulse was foolish. He wasn't dating George, and even if he were, he was well past the age of it being rational to fear a girlfriend's father. Once again, he glanced to the group of people she'd been with. "I guess I should let you get back to Tyler, and I'll go find—"

A tall man with graying hair appeared beside George, cutting off Bob's words. "Georgette, honey. I've been looking for you." The man turned to Bob. "I'm William Ecklington. Have we met before?" William shuffled his plate to his left hand, and extended his right.

Bob did the same, returning George's father's handshake.

"No. I don't believe we've met. I'm Bob Delanio."

"Pleased to meet you, Mr. Delanio." William's eyes flitted to Bob's off-the-rack suit, a sharp contrast to his tailor-made one. "I'm curious. How do you know my daughter?"

"I'm—"

"Daddy, why don't we sit down at one of the tables to talk? It's almost time for the speaker, and we should get good seats."

William frowned at her interruption, then turned back to Bob. "I suppose."

As they walked toward a free table, George turned quickly to him, and mouthed a word that looked like "help," which made no sense to Bob.

The second they were seated, George leaned toward her father. "Mr. Delanio is my boss, Daddy. He's the co-owner, with his partner."

William picked up a canapé and inspected it, replacing it on his plate before addressing Bob. "I haven't had much of a chance to talk to my daughter since she started working for your corporation. What is it exactly she does for you?"

"Uh…" While he and Bart had decided a few years ago to incorporate, they'd never thought of the tiny repair shop as a "corporation." "Well, your daughter is my…" Under the table, Bob felt a sharp tapping on his ankle, halting his words. He raised one hand to his mouth and pretended to cough to give himself some time to figure out why George was kicking him.

"Administrative assistant, Daddy. I'm positive I told you that before. Please, let's not talk so much business tonight. I hear these shrimp canapés are simply divine. You should go get more, before they run out."

Instead of leaving, William pushed his plate away.

"That's okay, I've had enough. Tell me, has my daughter been doing a good job for you?"

Bob picked up a shrimp canapé and popped it into his mouth, hoping that chewing would buy him some time to assimilate the image she wanted him to project. He'd never had an administrative assistant. He didn't even know what one did. George did the bookkeeping, which was the only office-type function needed.

"She handles all our accounting."

William frowned. "Accounting?"

Again, Bob felt a sharp tap on his ankle.

"Yes, but that's only a small part of her duties. George…" His words cut off at another sharp tap at his ankle.

"…ette," he continued, noting an almost inaudible sigh from George, "has been instrumental in expanding our customer base." He rubbed the spot with the top of his other foot. He wasn't wearing his safety boots. If the kicking didn't stop, he was going to have a very sore left foot.

William smiled, and when William smiled, George smiled, telling Bob that he was saying what they both wanted to hear.

He wasn't lying. Upon completion of all work orders, they routinely asked new customers how they'd found out about the shop. Lately, a number of people said a friend had been impressed by the new mechanic, and had recommended them. Reading between the lines, he knew a number of the younger, single men had simply come to check out the hot chick. Still, it was new business, and he had to give George the credit for it.

William leaned back in his chair. "I was very surprised she had taken a job. I'm glad she's doing well."

"Yes. She's been very good for the company."

"So, Mr. Delanio, what is it your company does?"

George's eyes opened farther than Bob had ever seen, and he could see the beginning of panic as her whole body went stiff.

Bob couldn't bear to watch her; he cleared his throat. "We deal mostly with the automotive industry. Because of your daughter, we're now in a position to expand." By adding another phone line.

"Ah." William nodded. "So it's a small company. My company began that way, of course, but it has never been small in *my* lifetime. The chain was founded by my grandfather, passed on through two generations. I'm chairman of the board now, but I insist on overseeing the area managers, who oversee the individual stores coast to coast. A smart businessman pays attention to details."

Bob's stomach lurched, and all the good food he'd eaten so far turned to a lump in his stomach. He recognized the name. He'd read in the financial section of the paper recently that William Ecklington's chain of department stores had topped sales from previous years, and the value of the stocks had taken an unprecedented jump.

Bob tried not to feel intimidated and failed. Of course he'd noticed her last name, but he'd never connected her with *those* Ecklingtons. He didn't understand why George was working for his pitiful little local garage when she came from such a wealthy family.

William stood. "If you'll excuse me, there are a number of other people I have to talk to. It's been a pleasure meeting you, Mr. Delanio. I hope to see you again at the next Chamber function."

Bob stood. "Usually it's my partner who attends these functions, but it's been a pleasure meeting you, too."

Bob shook William's hand and they parted company. He immediately turned to George, his plate of food forgotten.

George's lower lip trembled as her eyes widened. Her voice cracked as she spoke. "I suppose I owe you an explanation, don't I?"

Bob's voice lowered. "Yes, and I think we'd best go outside."

Chapter Eight

Georgette hadn't been looking forward to attending another function with Tyler, but never in her worst nightmares could she have foreseen what had just happened. She nodded, and followed Bob outside to the patio, to a bench at the edge of the deck, away from the other people who were also outside.

She sucked in a deep breath, held it for a few seconds, then exhaled deeply. "I don't know what to say."

Bob didn't respond.

Georgette didn't think that was a good sign.

"Am I fired?" she asked, trying to hold her voice steady.

"I don't know what to say either. I can't fire you when you're doing a good job. But I don't understand why in the world you're working at my little garage when you're an heiress. Don't you have something better to do with your time?"

"I need this job, but not for the reason you think." She paused, and lowered her voice. "My father is smothering me. I couldn't take it anymore."

Bob remained silent.

"I'm so sorry, Bob. I was afraid to tell you." She turned her head away, so he couldn't see her face. "But by waiting, I've only made it worse." Georgette stared off into the darkening night sky, and sighed. "I don't know if this is going to come out right. I know it makes me sound very ungrateful. I get all the financial benefits of being my father's daughter, but I'm so unhappy. My father refuses to give me a chance to prove myself or do anything worthwhile."

"Certainly there's a place for you somewhere in his corporation," Bob said wryly.

Georgette shook her head. "You'd think so, but he won't give me a chance. I even told him I'd go to university, but my father wouldn't pay for anything business or finance related. He said if I want to go to university, I have to take something in arts and sciences."

Bob stiffened. "When Bart and I first started the shop, I couldn't afford to go to university. My family helped me pay for a few business courses at the local community college. The rest I learned by experience, mostly the hard way."

Georgette hunched her shoulders and lowered her head. "My father has made it very clear he that he doesn't think either my sister or I are capable of running the business. He said once I get married, he'll make my husband a junior partner, or give him some kind of management job, like he did for my sister's husband, but other than that, he doesn't believe in husbands and wives working together. Or fathers and daughters. The only way I'll ever be a part of the business is to marry someone my father finds suitable, and hope he can convince my father to let me do something even as insignificant as filing. But I can't see that happening. Otherwise, the only other way is to wait until my father dies, and I inherit part of the business. I don't want either one to happen. I want to control my own future."

"And you think working as a junior mechanic is a bright future?"

She stared down at her shoes. "Maybe not. But at least I'm happy. I really feel God pointed me in the direction of your shop that day. At the end of the day I go home feeling as though I've done something to deserve my paycheck." Her voice dropped to a scratchy whisper. "The allowance my father gives me is a pay-off to be seen at his side like the family dog. I like to think I'm worth more than that."

"But he seemed happy that you're my administrative assistant, though it's a pretty lofty title within a three person operation."

Georgette still couldn't look at Bob and began to absently play with a leaf hanging near the armrest of the bench. "At first, he was angry that I even found a job, so I stretched the part about my function as your bookkeeper, and omitted the mechanic part. I meant to tell him, but for the first time in so long, he seemed really proud of me, watching me leave all dressed up to go to work in the morning. I later found out that it was because he thought I had taken a job in order to find a husband. By then it to was too late to tell him everything."

"So that's why you come to work all dressed up."

All she could do was nod.

He remained silent for a few minutes. "We should go back inside so we don't miss the speaker. I guess you're sitting with Tyler."

"Yes."

"What's up with Tyler, anyway? I can't figure out how he fits into this picture. He obviously knows you're working for me in a not-so-glamorous position."

"That's the point. He knows about my job, and he said he'll do me a favor and not tell my father if I help him make contacts to further his position."

"That's not a favor. That's blackmail."

"I know. But I don't have any other choice."

"But now your father has met me."

Georgette shook her head. "Nothing has changed. From what he sees, you're an executive, and I'm your administrative assistant. Now it seems I've only dug myself in deeper. I don't know what to do."

"There's a proverb from the Bible about that. I forget exactly how it goes, but it says that if you trap yourself by what you've said, then humble yourself and talk about it with that person, and don't wait. God gives us good advice. You tell me every Thursday how Tyler forces you to go places you don't want to be, and now I understand. So you didn't want to be here either, huh?"

Georgette looked at Bob. Her father thought the world of Tyler, even knowing Tyler often manipulated and coerced people and situations to get what he wanted. But Bob would never do that. Bob was ten times the man Tyler could ever be.

"You're right of course. I can't take much more of this. It's driving me crazy."

He stood, as did Georgette.

"Things like this drive me crazy, too. And on that note, we should take our seats." he said. "I probably won't see you until church Sunday night."

"Thanks, Bob. For everything."

He nodded, then walked away.

Georgette made it back to the table to sit with Tyler just as the master of ceremonies stepped up to the podium to make a few announcements and introduce the speaker.

Tyler leaned toward her. "Where have you been? I was beginning to think you'd left."

"Of course I didn't leave. My boss is here. I introduced him to Daddy, and then we had a few things to talk about."

"You're kidding, right?" Tyler made a snide laugh. "You introduced your father to that grease monkey?"

Georgette gritted her teeth. "Bob isn't a grease monkey. He's co-owner of a registered, incorporated business."

Tyler snorted. "Okay. He's a grease monkey with credentials. Come on, Georgette. Get serious."

"He's worked very hard to get where he is. Give him some credit."

"I don't extend credit to people like him."

"I don't need to listen to this. You've dragged me to enough of these things, more than I even originally agreed to. Our arrangement is over. And I think you—"

Her words were drowned out by the applause as the guest speaker approached the podium.

Throughout the entire presentation, Georgette's mind churned. All she could think about was how fast she could get out, and away from Tyler.

It was a relief when the audience applauded the close of the speaker's comments. Just as she reached under her chair for her purse, another voice sounded behind her.

"Georgette, honey. There you are."

"Daddy! You startled me."

"I was looking for your boss, Mr. Delanio, but I couldn't find him. I thought maybe he was with you."

"I think he went home."

"After we met, I made a few inquiries. No one seems to know who he is."

Georgette froze, then forced herself to smile graciously. "His company is very small."

"Exactly how small? Does he employ under fifty people?"

"Yes, it's well under fifty people. But it has good potential." She moved to get away, but her father blocked her path.

"I didn't recognize the family name, and no one I knew recognized the name, either."

"It's a first-generation company."

Georgette cringed as her father contemplated the implications. All his business associates were "old money." Even their new ventures weren't really "new," because they were financed with that "old" money.

Bob's parents were Italian immigrants, having come to the country shortly before he was born. His father worked in a blue-collar factory job, and still had many years before he could retire. Bob expected to do the same, a lifetime of long hours and hard work.

"It's okay, Daddy. The company is stable and has an established client base."

Tyler's laughter made Georgette flinch. "She's right on that issue, William. As long as there are middle class people with low class cars, Bob Delanio will always have an established client base."

"I don't understand."

"He's the Bob of Bob And Bart's Auto Repair."

"I've never heard of it."

"And you likely never will, either. It's not exactly a multi-national corporation."

"Tyler!" Georgette hissed. "What are you doing?"

Tyler made a self-satisfied snort. "You don't think that I just happened to appear in a neighborhood like that by accident, do you?"

"I don't understand."

"When your father said you got a job, I thought I'd find out what it was. No one seemed to know anything about it."

Georgette's heart turned cold. What she had suspected was now confirmed.

Tyler smirked. "I also did a little background check on your Bob and Bart. One look at their business history tells me that they only hired you for the potential financial backing you carry with your name."

"That's not true."

"Why else do you think they hired you? For your mechanical skills?"

"Yes!"

Beside her, her father gasped. "Mechanical skills?"

Tyler continued. "Didn't you think a background check would turn up who you were?"

"They don't have the money for a background check. They hired me because Bart knew the person I used as a reference on my résumé."

"Then they're fools."

"They're not fools. They're honest working men. And they trust people they associate with." Georgette bit her tongue. She knew her argument would go nowhere with Tyler. Tyler trusted no one. For that matter, neither did her father.

Her father held up his hand for silence. "What do you mean, mechanical skills? I spoke to Mr. Delanio. He said that Georgette was his administrative assistant."

Tyler spun around. "I don't know what Mr. Delanio calls an administrative assistant. All she does that's administrative is type up invoices for the repair work Mr. Delanio and his partner do. They're mechanics. Nothing more."

"That's not true. I do more than that."

All the color drained from her father's face. "You work for a couple of mechanics?"

Tyler's smirk returned. "She's right there. She does do more than type up invoices. She's also their spare mechanic."

"Spare mechanic?" her father sputtered, and then his face turned to stone. "Do you know what this looks like, my daughter accepting a job like that?" He buried his face in his hands. "My daughter is a *mechanic*. I'll be a laughingstock." He dropped his hands and glared at her. "How could you do this to me?"

"I didn't do anything *to* you. I did something *for* me for the first time in my life. No one has to know."

Her father waved one hand in the air, something he only did when he was very, very angry. "What were you thinking? Of course people will find out. Tyler found out."

Only because Tyler had been following her that day he first showed up at her job. His intent had been solely to curry favor with her father by relaying information about her. However, Tyler had discovered a better way to take advantage of his ill-found knowledge, much to her dismay. What she didn't understand was why Tyler had suddenly decided to divulge what he knew.

"Tyler has asked for your hand in marriage, who knows why. Even after what he knows, he'll still have you."

Her stomach sank like a rock. "Have me? That's not what marriage is all about! I can't marry Tyler."

"Yes, you can. And you will. You have disgraced our family name and my reputation. If he'll still have you, this is the only way to maintain my dignity."

"*Your* dignity?" She pressed her palms over her heart. "What about me?"

"You have shamed me. This is no longer about you."

"It's very much about me. This isn't the fifteenth century."

"Reputation is more important than anything, particularly in business. You will do as I say. Fortunately people have seen you together often lately, so you can set a date quickly."

Georgette's head spun. "I'm not marrying Tyler. I don't love him." She gritted her teeth. "I don't even like him." She turned and glared at Tyler. "We had a deal. You weren't going to tell my father what you knew, and in exchange I did what you wanted me to do. I can't believe I fell for it. People thought we were actually dating! I played right into your hands, didn't I?"

Tyler shrugged his shoulders. "This is really for your own good, Georgette. You can't believe that you have a future being a mechanic. Your rightful place is in society. You should be able to see that."

"All I see is that you're good at double-dealing. Now I trust you less than ever."

Her father stepped closer and crossed his arms. "I had a deal with Tyler first. He said he would find out exactly where you were working, and why you were being so evasive with me. He did exactly what he was supposed to do and what I would have done in his place. The ability to know when to turn the tables will take him far in business. And speaking of business, now I've met your 'boss,'" her father spat out the word with the utmost disdain, "you can't seriously believe his pathetic business has a future for you, or for our family. The only place you have a future is with Tyler. You will marry him, or...or...or I'll disown you."

Georgette grasped the edge of the table to steady herself. "You don't mean that."

"I've put up with your foolishness until now, but this job is the final straw. I've given you everything you wanted, and more, and now I find out that you're spending your time with some backwoods grease monkey! It's time for you to put your ridiculous ideas aside, and start doing things my way. You've forced my hand on this."

Georgette's entire life flashed before her eyes. It was true, she knew she'd been spoiled, but, except for the job, she'd always done everything her father desired.

"And from now on, I want you to attend Sunday-morning brunches either with me or with Tyler."

"But I go to church on Sunday mornings."

"Church is a crutch for people who are weak. You won't be going back there. Or to your job. Is this clear?"

Her voice trembled. "No, Daddy, it's not clear. Why are you doing this to me?"

His voice deepened. "You are an Ecklington. You don't need church. And you certainly don't need a job."

Perhaps she didn't need the job, but she did need church—and God—more than she ever had in her entire life. She knew God wouldn't turn His back on her if she didn't go to church on Sunday, but she had so much to learn, and she needed to be with other believers. Even though she could be close to God anywhere, she found it difficult when surrounded by decadence. Church was where she truly felt God's presence. God's presence wasn't exactly welcomed in her home.

Her father's voice broke into her thoughts. "I'm sending you home in the limo to give yourself time to think. I'll follow with Tyler. When we get there, I will hear your decision."

"My decision won't change," Georgette snapped. She scooped up her purse and stomped outside to the limo. The driver opened the door, she slid inside and the door closed, cutting her off from her father and the rest of the outside world. In the past, she'd always considered the limo a safe haven. Tonight, it suffocated her.

She turned around and watched through the rear window as Tyler and her father walked into the parking lot together.

They were a matched set. Tyler would do anything her father said, and anticipate his every need for the possibility of gaining his favor. Her father reveled in Tyler's adoration, which made Tyler expect even more from the relationship. Everyone knew where things were heading. Tyler would rise up quickly in the ranks of her father's empire.

Knowing Tyler, Georgette should have expected his duplicity. Not to see that he'd initially been acting on her father's instruction made her ten times the fool. But then, it was her own fault. It had been easier to believe what she wanted to believe and that had b been her downfall. She knew what Tyler was capable of doing. He acknowledged no guilt in taking advantage of her or forcing her hand in marriage.

It didn't matter what her father said or what threats he made. She would never marry Tyler. For any reason. Ever.

If she was going to marry someone, she would marry a man like Bob—a man who was honest and hard-working, and a wonderful example of how to lead a good life, with God in the middle of it.

The car stopped in front of the house instead of pulling into the garage.

She wondered if she could tell the driver to keep going, but the door opened, sending in a draught of cold air. Her father must have taken a short cut.

He released the door handle and stepped back. "What do you have to say for yourself?" he ground out between his teeth.

"Certainly you can't expect that I'm going to marry him," she pointed at Tyler as she scrambled out, "just because you don't approve of my job or the people I've been seeing lately."

"I most certainly do. For a long time, I've hoped that you would marry Tyler. He would fit well into the business, and our family. In fact, I'm considering a plum position for him right now, based on his dedication."

Tyler might have been a good match for the business and for their dysfunctional family, but not for Georgette's heart. After attending dozens of events since their "arrangement," she liked him even less than she had before. Now, after what he'd done today, he downright disgusted her. She certainly couldn't marry him. The only reason she would ever marry was for love.

She turned to her father. "Why did you marry Momma?"

"I married your mother because she was pregnant. Getting married was the right thing to do."

"Did you love her?" she choked out. They'd always been told Terri had been premature.

He cocked his head to the side. "Not really. But she loved me." He arched one eyebrow and turned to Tyler who smiled in response. "I was young and our parents saw to it that that we did what was expected. Everything was fine until your mother got all those ridiculous ideas in her head."

Georgette pressed her hand over the gold cross beneath her dress. She had a feeling she knew what he meant by "those ridiculous ideas," and wondered for the first time if her mother had really left, or if she'd been "disowned," to use her father's term, for her beliefs. It didn't matter.

Even if the reward was the smallest corner of her father's corporate world, she couldn't marry for any reason other than the love of a good man.

Like Bob. Not that she was in love with her boss, of course, she corrected herself.

She cleared her throat. "I already told you. I won't marry Tyler. Ever."

Her father extended one arm, drawing her attention to a stack of boxes stacked haphazardly on the grass. Clothing and some of her personal items from her bedroom stuck out at odd angles, telling her that the boxes had been packed in a hurry by his staff. A cold numbness started to overtake her. Georgette stepped forward, reached into one of the boxes, and pulled out the stuffed teddy bear that she kept on top of her bed.

"I'm giving you ten seconds to change your mind."

When her father had said he'd disown her, she hadn't thought he'd meant that he would kick her out immediately. This must be the same way her mother had disappeared in one afternoon.

Tyler's voice sounded behind her, every word echoing into her brain. "I'll be a good husband to you."

Her mouth opened, but no sound came out. Her father called himself a good husband, too, claiming the failure of the marriage was her mother's fault and nothing could be blamed on him. He'd kicked his wife out, and now he was kicking out his daughter.

"Your time is up. What's your decision?"

"I haven't changed my mind. I'm not going to marry Tyler, I'm not going to quit my job and I'm not going to quit going to church."

"You're no better than your mother." He pointed into the center of his chest. "I'm the one who brings in all the money. I'm the one who provides a home and all the perks that go with the fortune I bring into this house. I gave her anything she wanted. She had no right to refuse to do things my way. And neither do you!"

After experiencing a sample of what he considered publicly acceptable in order to get ahead, Georgette could only guess at his less public methods. "But what if what you're doing is wrong?"

His face turned red. "How dare you criticize me, after all I've done for you! Is this what that church does to you? Teach you to question my judgment and my success? Your mother was exactly the same. Get off my property. I no longer consider you an Ecklington."

Georgette stared at the pile of the boxes, not many, really, considering all the material items she considered hers, even though most of it had been paid for by her father. Her father had obviously instructed the staff to be very selective in order to keep what was "his" by purchase.

"And get that monstrosity you call a truck off my property, as well. If it's not gone by morning, I'm having it towed to the junkyard."

She turned to see that her truck was in the driveway,

not in the garage, where she had been storing it while she continued to work on it. In all the excitement, she hadn't noticed it. "But…" her voice trailed off.

"Don't try using any of your credit cards. They're all in my name, and I've cancelled them. Soon I will be removing all the money I have deposited in your account since that account has my name on it too. All that will remain is the money you've put in from your pathetic job. Less what you've spent in the past month, of course, if that leaves anything at all. I'm giving you one last chance to get some sense into your head and change your mind."

Georgette stiffened. "Never!"

"You have no idea what it takes to succeed in this world. No one will do anything for you without getting something in return, and you don't have what it takes to handle any kind of pressure. You won't survive. You'll be back, and when that happens you'll do things my way."

Her father turned, opened the door, and stepped into the house. Tyler followed him inside and the door closed.

Chapter Nine

Georgette stood, facing the closed door, unable to move.

The reflection of the moon on the smooth wood mocked her with its silence.

Everything she had taken for granted was gone.

Her car. Her computer. The furniture. Her jewelry. Her tools.

She still had her cell phone in her purse, but she was positive that by morning, that account would be terminated too.

She tried to imagine the contents of her closet, her dresser and the racks of shoes. She couldn't imagine everything stuffed into only a dozen boxes, but that was all that remained. Her life had been reduced to a dozen boxes, sitting on the lawn.

Money can't buy happiness.

She didn't need so much money. All that money certainly hadn't bought her a trouble-free life.

But love doesn't pay the rent.

Georgette squeezed her eyes shut. She didn't have to

worry about paying the rent. She didn't have a home to pay rent on.

But she would. She refused to go crawling back to her father, and do the wrong thing for the wrong reasons.

For years, she'd wanted to become independent, and now she was going to do it.

She pulled her keyring out of her purse, removed the key to her father's car and the key to the front door, and left them on the doormat, which she would never cross again. She kicked off her high-heeled shoes and loaded the boxes into the back of her truck, one at a time.

The truck didn't start easily, but it did start. Fortunately she'd insured it so she could take it on test drives as she continued to work on it. The insurance was one thing her father couldn't cancel.

She drove away from her father's home without looking back.

She didn't know where to go. Without looking, she knew she had under five dollars in her wallet.

Her first impulse was to go to the bank machine, but by the time she got there, her father's threats had indeed come to pass. He'd gone into the account online and transferred out all the money he'd given her, just as he'd said he would. Of course, since she'd counted on her allowance, she'd spent more than what she'd received in her pay. The account now held exactly one dollar, which was probably the minimum requirement to keep the account open.

She couldn't seek shelter at the homes of any of her current friends. She wasn't even sure she could call them friends. She hadn't seen a single one of them since she'd started her job, and not one of them cared enough to ask about her. Not one of them would ever do anything to cross her father.

The people she called friends were the guys at the race track. Yet those friendships were minor ones, not true personal relationships. No one there knew her background, and she worked hard to keep it that way. Many of them lived from paycheck to paycheck, and she didn't want to intimidate them. Besides, most of them were married and so she couldn't very well show up at the home of a married man on Friday night, asking to spend the night. She certainly wouldn't ask any of the single men that question.

Another option would have been the people she knew from church, but she didn't know anyone well enough to impose. The only people she'd had minimal contact with were those in the family from whom she'd bought the truck, and they had enough problems of their own without adding hers. Lately she hadn't even been going to her own church. Instead, she'd been sneaking into Bob's church, arriving late because of the long drive, and leaving right at the close of the service. Bob never even knew she was there, but she needed to get home before her father became too angry with her for going to church at all.

For lack of anywhere else to go, Georgette drove to her sister's house. Her sister wouldn't agree with what she'd done, but she would certainly understand. Whatever Terri thought, Georgette needed someplace safe and warm to retreat for the night, a quiet place to think about her future.

She knocked softly at the door and heard shuffling, then silence. Georgette waited for a significant amount of time, and when no one answered, she knocked again.

"Terri? Are you there? Byron? It's me. Georgette. Please let me in."

More shuffling sounded on the other side of the door, and then it opened.

Her brother-in-law stood in the doorway, his clothing disheveled. "What are you doing here at this hour?"

She looked down at her watch, then back up again. "It's not really that late, but…" Georgette's voice trailed off.

Romantic music echoed in the background, but Terri was nowhere to be seen. A bottle of wine sat on the coffee table, with two half-empty glasses beside it. A pair of ladies' shoes lay on the carpet beside the couch. Pretty shoes, but they were big. Not her sister's size fives.

"Terri isn't home. Is there something you need?"

"Where is she?"

"She was out with Melissa, shopping all day. They went out for dinner and the evening, and she's spending the night downtown with Melissa."

A sick feeling gripped her stomach. Georgette glanced from side to side. Along with the faint smell of the wine, she could smell a woman's perfume.

"May I come in?"

"Actually, I'm really tired, so this isn't a good time. I'll tell Terri you were here."

For the second time that night, a door closed in her face.

This time, instead of standing there and staring at the closed door, Georgette turned and ran straight for her truck. She drove away quickly, without thinking of where she was going.

She found herself in the parking lot of the repair shop.

She slid out of the cab and stood in the lot, empty except for her pickup, and stared up at the decidedly non-glamorous, board sign, lit up by a pair of colored spotlights. In the darkness, the old building looked even more drab than usual, but at least the night hid the marred surface where vandals had once written crude words, though Bart had cleaned most of it off.

It wasn't much, but she had nowhere else to go. Payday was six days away. She had less than half a tank of gas, almost no money in her wallet, no credit cards, and no one left to turn to.

A cool breeze caused her to shiver.

Without digging through the boxes, she wasn't sure she even had a jacket.

She ran her fingers along the keys in her hand. About a week ago, Bob had given her a key and the alarm code, saying that in case of an emergency, she might need to come in early, or lock up one night.

This might not be an emergency in the strictest sense of the word, but the shop was her only safe haven for shelter and warmth for the night.

She said a quick prayer that she'd remembered the code correctly, and opened the door. Just as Bob had warned her, the system started with a series of beeps. She quickly pushed the code into the buttons on the keypad, and the building went silent.

While the shop was located on a commercial roadway, in this end of town it wasn't exactly a major thoroughfare. She stood still, experiencing the silence as never before. Her father's house was often silent when her father and all the staff were sleeping at night, but she was always comforted by knowing they were there.

Here, though everything was familiar, she felt truly alone.

She turned and stared outside. A few cars were lined up along the fence, waiting their turn to be fitted into the work schedule, but her old truck was the only vehicle in the parking lot. She trusted the neighborhood in the daytime, when everything was bustling with activity, but at night, if someone came by and wanted to steal the last of her worldly belongings, from the back of the truck, she would be helpless to do anything. By the time she could call the police, they would be gone.

She caught the reflection of herself in the large window. She was still wearing her new dress, the one the same color as Bob's eyes. She could do nothing about that. But she could do something about her footwear. She kicked off her high-heeled shoes, retrieved her safety workboots and an extra pair of wool socks from beneath the counter, and slipped them on.

Depending only on the muted light from the streetlamps, Georgette hauled all twelve boxes into the corner of the private office without turning on the light so anyone passing by wouldn't think she was taking things out instead of moving things in, and call the police. Once all the boxes were inside, she moved her truck to the lineup of vehicles along the fence.

When she was done, Georgette locked the door behind her and sank down on the worn couch.

She'd couldn't remember ever being so tired. It was now Saturday, 4:48 a.m. She'd been up at 6:15 a.m. on Friday morning in order to get ready and be at work for 8:00 a.m. She'd put in a full eight hours on the job, and then when she got off, she'd gone shopping for the new dress she'd worn to that fateful Chamber of Commerce banquet. Then she'd moved whatever remained of her material possessions twice, first lifting everything into the back of her truck, then carrying everything inside the building.

The chill of the night started to set into her bones now that she was sitting still. Being tired made everything feel worse. She hoped that whoever threw her things into the boxes had included a jacket or a sweater. If she couldn't find a sweater, then she could grab any article of clothing and throw it around her shoulders like a shawl.

Except she didn't have the energy to move to find out.

Georgette wrapped her arms around herself, and let her head fall back on the couch.

Her life was a disaster. But, for now, she had a roof over her head and a clean washroom nearby, which was all that mattered until daylight.

When the sun began to rise, that would be her signal to leave. Like most people, she worked Monday to Friday, but Bob worked six days a week, including Saturdays and since it was now officially Saturday morning, Bob would soon be in to open for business though a little later than the weekday opening.

Not bothering to fight back a yawn, she tried to figure out what she could do until it was time to sneak off. No thoughts would form, so she did the only thing she could think of, which was to ask God for help.

No answer came.

Slowly, the world faded to black.

Bob tucked the morning newspaper under his arm while he unlocked the door, then pushed it open. He stepped inside and flipped the panel covering to turn off the alarm, ready to punch in the code, but his hand froze in mid-air.

There was no tell-tale beeping that the door had been opened or that the motion detector had caught his presence.

He blinked and stared at the panel. The green light was on, not the red.

Slowly, he tapped his chin with the rolled-up newspaper as he continued to stare at the panel. He had been the last one out on Friday night. If he'd forgotten to set the alarm in his hurry to get home and change for the banquet, then this was another sign that he was working too hard. That was the reason they'd hired George, but they'd obviously hired her too late. He was already losing it.

He began to turn around, then stopped. As if she'd materialized from his thoughts, George lay on the couch in the lobby.

Bob shook his head, but the image didn't clear.

Still in a sitting position, she was sprawled on the couch, her head resting at what had to be a painful angle, her blond hair spread like a halo around her face. She still wore her dress from Friday night, a close-fitting, silky green number that proved there was more to George under those coveralls than just a mechanic.

But the worn workboots on her feet shouted exactly that.

She gave a little snort, her head jerked slightly as if to awaken, then sagged once more.

Bob ran his fingers though his hair and looked outside. The parking lot was empty at 7:30 a.m., except for his own car. So he wasn't totally losing his mind by not realizing she was there before he stepped inside. But that only added to the mystery of how she got there, especially since George was dressed as though she hadn't been home.

Very quietly, he approached her until he was only one step away. He waited, but she didn't awaken.

Bob leaned forward and sniffed the air. He didn't detect the smell of alcohol, only her perfume.

He closed his eyes as he inhaled the faint but heady scent more deeply. He knew it was only the expensive perfumes that could linger for hours and hours and remain sweet, but now that he knew who she was, that she could spend so much money on perfume didn't surprise him.

Bob quickly stepped backward and opened his eyes at the memory.

She was no longer just George the mechanic. This was Georgette Ecklington, daughter of William Ecklington, billionaire magnate of the biggest chain of retail discount stores in the country.

And she was sleeping on his couch. His old, beat-up, dirty couch that he'd repaired with duct tape.

Suddenly, her eyes opened. She blinked a few times, gasped and scrambled to her feet.

Her eyes lost their focus, and she began to sway.

Without thinking, Bob grasped her shoulders to keep her from falling.

After a few seconds, she raised one hand and pressed her fingers between her brows. "I think I stood up too fast."

"Are you okay?"

She nodded, so Bob released her, and stepped back once more. "What are you doing here? Where's your car?" He looked down at the workboots on her feet. *And your shoes…*

Her lower lip trembled. "I don't have a car. But I have a truck…" She turned her head and Bob followed her motion with his. Parked in the row of vehicles waiting their turn for repairs, was an old, decrepit pickup truck he didn't recognize.

Her voice shook as she spoke. "That truck is mine."

"But it's so…" he let his voice trail off. He really didn't care about what she drove, although the condition surprised him. His main concern was George. "You didn't tell me what you're doing here." He knew she'd been to the banquet with Tyler, and an urge to protect George boiled to the surface. Bob clenched his fists. If Tyler had hurt her or threatened her to cause her to hide, Bob didn't care who Tyler was, or where he lived. Bob would force him to make it right.

George's voice came out in a choked volume barely above a whisper. "I had nowhere else to go."

"I don't understand."

"I told Daddy I wouldn't marry Tyler."

Bob shook his head. "Now I really don't understand. I think I've missed something."

"It started at the banquet, after you left. Tyler told Daddy everything. Daddy didn't take it very well."

While she paused, Bob looked down at her. Despite the snug fit, George's dress was wrinkled. Besides that, it was smudged with dirt, almost as if she'd been rolling on the ground. He followed a run in her pantyhose that extended from beneath the rolled edge of the wool socks visible above her workboots, upwards, disappearing past the hemline of her dress.

Bob quickly raised his eyes. "Tyler asked you to marry him?"

"Not really. But he discussed it with Daddy. Daddy told me I had to marry Tyler because I had ruined the family name and his reputation. Daddy actually approved of what Tyler was doing."

"Now I know I'm confused. Maybe you should go back to the beginning."

"After you met my father, Tyler told him what you really do, and what I really do for you. Daddy was mortified, to put it mildly. He said that his reputation would be ruined, and the only way to save it was for me to marry Tyler. But I refused. So Daddy kicked me out."

"He kicked you out because you won't marry someone you don't love?" Suddenly he didn't want to be looking into her face, just in case she said she did love Tyler. It shouldn't have made a difference to him, but it did.

He lowered his head, intending simply to stare at the floor, but he found himself staring again at her workboots. The workboots belonged to George the mechanic. The woman before him was wealthy beyond anything he could ever imagine. At the banquet, he'd thought she looked spectacular in that dress, but now he knew why. That dress was probably worth an entire month's mortgage payment. Yet now, with it, she was wearing dirty, worn workboots.

He didn't know which was the real George—the one wearing the workboots, or the one wearing the expensive dress.

"Of course I don't love Tyler. I don't know if this is a very Christian thing to say, but I think I actually hate him. Although I can't blame him entirely for what happened. I had planned to tell my father about what I really do here at some point, but I would have used better timing. In a different setting, he still would have been angry about my job, but I don't think he would have kicked me out."

"Your father kicked you out because you have a job?" Bob knew many families where the parents were ready to kick out lazy grown children because they *didn't* have a job.

"He was fine with me having a job, as long as it was the job I led him to believe, which is something with a title." She grinned. "Administrative assistant sounds good, don't you think?"

He couldn't help but grin back. "I guess. But I still don't know what one does."

Her playful grin dropped. "Not working with your hands and getting dirty, that's for sure. I love my job, but more than the job, I love doing what I want to do. I don't know if I'm being ungrateful for all my father has given me, but I want to make my own choices, especially when lately he's been trying to push everything down my throat. Not just getting married to Tyler, but his antiquated ideas of what I'm allowed to do and what I should be doing to make him look good. I just never realized being independent would come at such a high cost." Her voice lowered. "I don't think marrying Tyler, especially this way, is what God wants me to do with my life."

"What are you going to do?"

"I don't know. I'm so sorry, I know I shouldn't be here, but I had nowhere else to go, and I didn't know what to do."

"I think the first thing you need to do is start looking for an apartment."

"I can't. I don't have anything."

He unrolled the newspaper, which had been in his hand for so long some of the ink had come off on his skin. "Then a room-and-board situation would probably suit you. You could take your time buying new furniture if you don't mind smaller living quarters and sharing a bathroom." Although, knowing now the money-eyed background from which she'd come, he had no doubt she'd lived in quite a mansion. Not only were the grounds probably like living in a park, the house itself must have been huge and luxurious. Her bedroom was probably bigger than the living room in his humble house. Between carrying the mortgage on the house and half the mortgage payment on the business, he could afford to live comfortably no matter how small his house was in comparison to hers. That was all that mattered.

He walked to the coffee table, opened the newspaper and started paging through to the classified section. "I know how much you make, so I know what you can afford. I'm sure we can find something for you." He paused for a second, halting on his own words. He'd said *we,* and as soon as the word had come out of his mouth, he'd realized he meant it. Besides the fact that he liked her as a person, he felt somewhat responsible for her having been kicked out.

"I don't think you understand. I don't have any money until payday."

Bob looked up. "I don't know how personal I should get here, but let's define 'no money.' Just how low should I start looking? Some of these places aren't in the best neighborhoods, and you don't want to be there."

"I have $4.37."

"Anyplace will take a check, George. That's how most people pay the rent."

"No, you really don't understand. I have $3.37 in my wallet and exactly one dollar in my bank account. Daddy took back my allowance. I didn't see this coming, and I had lots of money last week when I went shopping. Daddy took out everything except for what I deposited myself, and he didn't leave anything to cover what I'd spent. That means everything I bought came out of my paychecks. My credit cards have been cancelled. Even my cell phone doesn't work anymore." She buried her face in her hands. "It's really starting to hit me now. Everything is gone. I don't even know what's in the boxes, I'm too afraid to look."

"Boxes?"

"The staff tossed my personal things in boxes, and dragged them outside. Everything I have left that my father doesn't think is rightfully his is in twelve boxes, which are stored in the corner of the private office until I can figure out what to do." Her stomach growled, causing her to cover her stomach with her arms. "I'm hungry, and I don't even have enough money for breakfast."

"Actually, you can buy a loaf of bread and a small jar of peanut butter with what you've got in your wallet, so technically, you do. But that doesn't solve your problems."

Bob raised his hand and ran his fingers through his hair again. He'd never been without support. His family didn't have much money, but they'd always had enough food to eat, a roof over their heads, each other, and God watching over them, and that was all that mattered.

When he'd started his business, his parents had cosigned the mortgage for the shop because the bank had turned him down. His family had been there to help when he needed it. By the time he bought his house, the business was stable enough that he could get a mortgage as a single person without a cosigner.

He studied George. By her drawn expression, he could tell she hadn't had enough sleep. The dark color of the dress made her look even paler.

Her stomach growled again. Instead of blushing, as most women did, her eyes became glassy. She blinked repeatedly, then swiped the back of her hand over them.

Bob's throat tightened. He reached into his back pocket, pulled out his wallet, and handed her some money. "Here. Go to the deli and bring back a couple of breakfast sandwiches."

"I can't accept your money."

"Don't worry about it. I said to buy two, one for you and one for me. It's just two friends sharing brunch together. You can pay next time." He really didn't want her to repay him, but he had a feeling that she would, even though she wouldn't be able to save the money for extras any time soon.

"Thank you," she muttered as she accepted his money. She took one step toward the door and skidded to a halt. She looked down at herself. "I can't go like this. Excuse me." She spun around and ran into the private office, and the door closed.

Instead of standing and staring at the door, Bob turned on the lights, flipped the sign to Open and booted up the computer. Just as he started to type in his password, George emerged from the office dressed in what he was more accustomed to seeing her wear—jeans and a T-shirt…and the workboots.

She looked down at her feet, and tapped her toes. "I couldn't find my sneakers, but I'm not about to wear dress shoes with jeans. I'll be right back." As Bob watched, she nearly skipped out the door, despite the heaviness of the steel-toed safety boots.

Instead of starting the day's projects, he returned to the newspaper and started looking for a room-and-board rental in a respectable neighborhood. He could only find a few vacancies that he considered reasonable, but none of them were in a neighborhood he approved of, especially knowing her background.

By the time she returned, Bart had arrived and Bob had joined him to work in the shop.

"She's back. I gotta go for a sec."

Bart straightened and rested his fists on his hips. "Who's back? George? What's she doing here on Saturday? You didn't tell me she was coming in. Is she taking time off another day, or are we paying her overtime?"

"Neither. It's personal."

A smile lit Bart's face. "Wow. I knew it."

"Don't even think about it. It's not that kind of personal. I'll be right back."

He could feel Bart's eyes on his back as he exited the shop and joined George in the office. She already had both sandwiches, complete with napkins, spread out on the counter.

Just as they did when they went out for dinner on Thursday nights, Bob led with a short prayer. George immediately bit into her sandwich as Bob took a glance at the logo on the wrapper. "I see you went to the deli, after all. You were gone so long I thought you took a trip across town."

She shook her head, then swallowed her mouthful with a big gulp. "I decided to walk in order to save gas. Also, while I was walking it gave me some time to think. If I could find a place to rent that's close to here, I could walk to work and cancel the insurance on my truck. I could use the refund to pay for a damage deposit, and maybe the rest for the balance of this month's rent. Did you find anything in the paper?"

"No, I didn't. Maybe I can get my mother to ask around and see if anyone she knows wants to take in a boarder—just until you can get on your feet financially. I'm sure that in a few months…" His words trailed off as a thought struck him.

"Bob? Is something wrong?"

"You're going to need a place to stay tonight, and my mother will never come up with something that quickly. But I may have another solution, at least a temporary one. A couple of years ago I fixed up my garage into a small apartment for when my cousin Jason was going to college. I've been using it for storage lately, but I'm sure it wouldn't take much to get it livable again. There's just one thing."

"It sounds perfect!"

Bob raised one hand. "I'm not finished explaining yet. When I said small, I meant really small. It's a regular single garage, but narrower inside because I insulated it and put up wallboard. It's basically one room with a living space on one end, and a utility kitchen on the other, outfitted like a camper. I made a small bathroom in one corner. There isn't even room for a bathtub, just a shower. Jason used a wardrobe in the corner to hang his clothes. You'd have to sleep on the futon which serves as a couch during the day and pulls out into a bed at night. It's not glamorous, but Jason liked it that way. It's easy to keep clean and besides, the biggest factor for him as a student was that it was free. If you want it, it's free to you, too, for as long as you want to use it."

George's eyes narrowed, and one corner of her mouth turned up. Bob could tell she was trying to imagine the garage apartment as he'd described it, except he doubted she really was aware of how small *small* could be. While she was on her way to the deli, he had pulled out her personnel file to look up her address. He hadn't known where she lived because George's first duty was to handle the paperwork and get the accounting caught up, so she had entered her own records into the computer, with their payroll of one.

The second he saw her father's address, he could picture the neighborhood. They weren't just homes. They were estates. Not a one would have a single-car garage. He wondered if she'd even ever *seen* a single-car garage.

"I still think it sounds perfect. Thank you so much. I don't know how I'll ever repay you."

Bob cleared his throat. "Don't worry about it, but maybe you should see it before you make up your mind."

Chapter Ten

Georgette followed Bob's car through the neighborhood to his house.

The homes were older and were all small and similar in design and structure. Yet, despite their age none were run down. Bob had explained to her that many of the residents were couples like his parents, who had bought the homes many years ago when they were first married, and had remained after their children were grown and gone. Lawn care had replaced child care for them over time.

Other residents were like Bob—first-time home buyers who purchased a small, older home because that was what they could afford.

Still, the neighborhood had a charm of its own, and Georgette didn't feel threatened, only out of place.

At the end of the block, Bob turned into a lane, and she followed.

With the age of the neighborhood, instead of built-in garages like her father's these homes had detached garages, accessible via a back lane.

Bob turned to park on a slightly raised cement pad beside a very small garage. Georgette slid out of her truck at the same time as he exited his own car, and she joined him.

"Here we are. Welcome home."

All Georgette could do was stare. The building was small. She couldn't see that there would be much room inside it for anything besides an average-sized vehicle. The gardener's shed on her father's property was bigger than Bob's garage.

She struggled to think of living in such a tiny building, but Bob's cousin had done exactly that for an entire school year. Therefore, so could she. Besides, beggars couldn't be choosers. It was either this, or go back to being a prisoner for the rest of her life. Like her father, Tyler would do everything in his power to limit her exposure to church and to other believers, and would do everything he could to squelch her faith in order to mold her into what he wanted her to be. She couldn't live like that.

Living in a building smaller than her bedroom at her father's house was fine, if it gave her the freedom to live her own life and make her own choices. She had to live the way God wanted her to live, not the way Tyler wanted.

Bob's ears turned red. "I'd like to say it looks better from the inside than from outside, but since I didn't have any notice, today it probably doesn't."

Georgette forced herself to smile graciously and told herself the same thing she'd thought just before she fell asleep on the couch in the lobby of the shop. It was a roof over her head and it had a clean washroom. At least she hoped the washroom was clean.

"I'm sure it's fine. I don't know what to say, you're being so generous."

His ears turned even redder. "Don't give credit where

it isn't due. It's not going to cost me anything for you to live here. I just have to find someplace else to put my junk."

She knew he was wrong, but she didn't want to argue with him and diminish his graciousness. At the very least, he would be paying more on his utility bill for the electricity she used.

He led her away from the roll-up door to a small, painted door on the side of the building, the entrance to her new home. No polished, carved mahogany double doors here.

"You don't have to worry about anyone getting in by opening the main garage door," Bob mumbled while he picked through his keyring. "The roll-up door opens, but I built a small storage area there. From the inside, it's a solid wall."

Georgette turned her head and looked from one end of the garage to the other. It was already small enough without taking away interior space for storage accessible only from the outside.

The door opened with a creak.

"I guess I'll have to oil that. Come on in. Just remember that I wasn't expecting anyone actually to be here."

"Oh!" she exclaimed, then slapped her hands over her big mouth. It was even smaller inside than she had imagined, although Bob had been perfectly honest about its shortcomings.

"Yeah. I know. It's really small."

Besides a number of boxes piled up, the only furniture inside was a futon, the smallest wardrobe unit she'd ever seen, a desk, a half-size kitchen table with two chairs and a small stand with a thirteen-inch television on top. It wasn't much furniture, but nothing else would fit and still leave room to walk. "It's okay. It's...cozy."

"It won't look so bad once all my extra stuff is out of here." He picked up a box and carried it outside, so Georgette did the same. When all the boxes were outside, they moved her twelve boxes from the back of her truck inside, making it look exactly the same, except that this time, the boxes were hers.

Bob swiped one finger through the layer of dust on the desktop. "This isn't bad, considering that no one has lived here for a year. You'll probably want to clean up before you start unpacking. Just let me stack my boxes in the storage area, and I'll go into my place and see what I can find. This will give you some time to check the place out on your own."

Before Georgette could protest, he was gone.

This was it. Her new home.

It felt like a closet with furniture. And lots of dirt.

She walked to what could loosely be defined as the kitchen. The refrigerator and stove were miniature versions, like those that might be found in a child's playhouse. Yet as small as they seemed, the size was appropriate to the rest of the dwelling. For the balance of the kitchen, one double-sized upper cabinet hung on the wall, and a double-sized lower cabinet with a countertop on it had been installed beside the fridge, half of the surface was taken up by a small sink. Even combined, the usable cupboard space wouldn't hold much, but Georgette had no idea what to put in them, anyway. She didn't know how to cook anything without a microwave oven, which was glaringly absent from the facilities. She didn't want to think about there being no dishwasher. But it didn't really matter. She didn't have any dishes.

A few steps further, she stepped into the doorway of

what had to be the bathroom, if the word *room* could be applied to a space so small.

Aside from the layer of dust, it looked relatively clean. To her surprise and delight, it was in much better condition than the washroom at the gas station where she changed her clothes every day.

"Well? What do you think?" Bob's voice echoed from behind her.

Her breath caught. She spun around, pressing her hands over her pounding heart.

"Oops. I didn't mean to scare you. I thought you heard me coming."

"No, I didn't. Everything looks good, except the toilet is broken. There's no water in it."

Bob grinned, then squeezed past her and knelt beside the toilet. He reached between it and the small vanity and turned a small chrome tap.

The trickling sound of running water resounded throughout the small room.

"That's because I turned the water off when Jason moved out. I didn't want it to stain."

"Stain?" She suppressed a shudder. "Is there something wrong with your water?"

"No, but if no one is using the toilet, the water would go stagnant from not being flushed for months, and would stain the bowl as it slowly evaporated over time. So it was just best to leave it dry."

The water stopped running. Bob turned and pushed the toilet handle, making it flush. She stared, fascinated, as the dry, empty bowl filled with clean water.

Georgette tried to stop the sinking feeling that threatened to envelop her. Her life had deteriorated to the point where she was happy to see a toilet flush.

"See? It works just fine. All this place needs is a good wipe-down and it'll be as good as new. I brought over a box of cleaning stuff and my vacuum cleaner for you to use. Now, if you'll excuse me, I should get back to work. I'll see you in a couple of hours."

Bob parked his car on the cement pad beside the garage where he always parked, but today he looked at it from a different perspective.

There was a second vehicle parked here.

George's.

By now, George was probably nearly finished making his garage into her home.

He grabbed the bag with the two burgers he'd picked up at the drive-through on his way home, and slid out of the car. As he did, Bart's words of caution came back to haunt him.

Earlier, when he got back to the shop, he'd had a long talk with Bart. Bart had reminded him that it wasn't a great idea to have their employee living on his property. Bob had agreed, but he couldn't put her out on the street. George was a Christian sister who needed help, and he had the means to provide it. This also changed everything about their relationship, the parameters of which he still hadn't fully considered.

He pushed the car door closed and started walking toward the garage. Now that she was living closer than next door, he wondered if she would be attending church with him in the morning; he wanted her to be there with him. So far she'd been attending the evening services, but he thought she'd been continuing to attend at her home church for the morning services, though someone had mentioned to him they'd seen her at his church.

Now that she was so close, things could be different. However, he wasn't sure that would be wise. In his current position, he should have been setting firm lines to distance himself. Instead, the lines were becoming more fuzzy. Yet, he couldn't not take her if she asked, even if the only reason to go to his church, the closer one, was because she didn't have any money for gas.

As he approached the side door, he noticed that it was wide open. When he stepped into the opening, the scent of pine cleaner was so strong it made his eyes water.

Bob stepped back to give himself some air.

"George?"

She didn't reply, but he could hear splashing coming from the bathroom, as well as the noise of the fan. Since the bathroom door was also wide open, he considered it safe to continue inside.

The closer he got, the stronger the onslaught of pine became, until his eyes wouldn't stop watering. He swiped his eyes with the back of his hand, and stepped into the opening for the bathroom.

He found George wringing out the sponge in the bathroom sink.

"What are you doing in here?"

"I'm finally done. What do you think?"

He blinked repeatedly, but his eyes still burned. "It looks good, but I think the smell of the cleaner is a bit overpowering."

"The label said it would make everything fresh and clean. It's antibacterial."

Bob swiped his hand over his eyes again, and resisted the urge to cough. "That could be, but I think you used a little too much."

George looked up at him, her eyes as red as his felt.

"The label said to use full strength on bathroom fixtures, and then diluted on wood and painted surfaces. So I did."

He looked at the bottle, which was on the floor next to the toilet. Before today, he'd only used it once. It was now half empty.

He turned toward the shower stall. Part of him wanted to see how shiny she'd scrubbed the inside, but part of him didn't want to open it, for fear of getting knocked out by the fumes.

Bob cleared his throat. "I brought supper. We should eat before it gets cold." Or permeated with pine. He would never again feel the same about walking through an evergreen forest.

They walked to the kitchen area. The sink, counters and appliances were so clean they sparkled, but the smell of pine wasn't diminished enough for Bob to want to expose his food to it. "Let's go into my house. I have ketchup."

He didn't give her a chance to respond. He simply walked out, expecting her to follow, which she did. Once outside, he inhaled deeply. When he did, the sudden ability to draw in unscented oxygen made his head spin.

"We should leave the door open, to air the place out while we're gone. We can keep an eye on everything from the kitchen."

All she did was nod, so Bob continued into his house. "It's kind of messy. I know I already said this earlier, but I wasn't exactly expecting company today. It's been a long, busy week, and housework isn't my first priority."

"That's okay."

Fortunately for Bob, he didn't have to lead her past his bedroom. The only time he made the bed was when he knew in advance that his mother was coming. The first thing she did when she arrived was march to his bedroom to check that he'd made the bed. When he hadn't, which was every time he wasn't expecting her, she promptly lectured him. Now, he wished he'd listened to her.

George wiped her hands down the sides of her jeans. "If you don't mind, I need to wash my hands. I can still smell that cleaner."

He pointed down the hall, hoping she wouldn't look into other rooms as she walked by. When she returned, she still smelled as if she'd been attacked by a pine tree, but he kept that thought to himself.

She joined him at the table, where he had already set a burger and fries in front of each of them, and poured them both a glass of milk. "I hope you're hungry."

George smiled weakly. "Actually, I'm not sure how I feel. I was so busy cleaning I didn't think about eating. I hope I did it right."

"I'm sure you did fine. Let's pray now, before this gets completely cold." He bowed his head, and said a short prayer, thanking God for both the meal and George's new home, and he began to eat.

George sat there glassy-eyed staring at the burger.

Bob stopped chewing. "What's wrong?"

She blinked and picked up the burger. "I feel so strange about this. You bought me lunch and now supper, and I don't have any way to repay you. More than that, you've given me a place to stay, rent-free. I've never had to accept someone's charity before, and I can't say I like it very much. I wish there was something I could do to repay you."

He shrugged his shoulders. "Don't worry about it. I already told you it's not a big deal. It's not costing me anything for you to stay in my garage. Although, now that you've cleaned it up, we should call it an apartment." He smiled.

She didn't smile back.

"It's okay, George. I'm sure there's something you can do for me. How about if we make it your job to sweep up the shop at the end of the day?"

She shook her head. "No. You already pay me a wage for stuff like that. I want to do something else for you."

"It looks like you did a good job cleaning the, uh, apartment. How about if you did some housecleaning for me?"

"Are you sure? I've never done this kind of thing before. I'm still not sure I did a good job."

"I'm sure you did." Even if she did use a double dose of the pine cleaner. Or maybe even a quadruple dose. They'd been away from the garage for ten minutes, and the pine forest still surrounded her. "Now eat your dinner. Good food makes everything better." He grimaced. "My mother always says that. I can't believe I'm repeating something my mother said."

She gave him a weak smile, and finally took a bite out of her burger. "Is your mother a good cook?"

"Yeah. She makes the best osso buco in the world. My brother Tony runs an Italian restaurant, and even he can't make osso buco like Mama. When she goes to his restaurant, she always ends up in the kitchen improving the recipes. I know that probably doesn't sound very good, but once you meet my mother, you'll understand." As soon as he realized what he'd said, he snapped his mouth shut.

He had already crossed the line between business and

personal too many times. He didn't need to expound on his mother and her quirks. It was bad enough that he was with George now, in his home.

After eating half the burger, George laid it on the wrapper. "I'm sorry, but I can't finish this." She paused and pushed the burger away. "Actually, I don't feel very good. At first I thought I was hungry, but now that I've eaten, I think I feel worse." She covered her mouth with her hand, and made a little cough.

Bob frowned. "I wonder if it's because you've inhaled too many fumes today. Maybe you should lie down."

She shook her head and took a long sip of milk. "I shouldn't need to do that. Josephine never has to lie down."

"Josephine?"

"Our housekeeper. She's very thorough. The house smells so nice and clean when she's finished every day. She always has Daddy's clothes freshly pressed so they're ready for him in the morning. Daddy likes to get into a warm shirt in the morning."

"Morning? She irons in the morning? You mean you had a live-in housekeeper?"

She blinked a few times. "Of course…"

Bob ran his fingers through his hair. He felt as though he'd been living in another universe light years away from George's world. "George, I've never even had a housekeeper, never mind a live-in person. I also wash my own floors and clean my own bathroom and do my own laundry."

"Why don't you send your laundry to the service that does the shop?"

"We don't *have* a service. On Saturday, Bart takes the bag of dirty coveralls home, and his wife washes everything for us. If you were wondering about who empties the garbage cans and washes down the bathrooms, Bart and I take turns. We alternate weekends."

Her face paled suddenly. As much as he didn't like housecleaning, Bob didn't think the concept was that abhorrent. He accepted it as something that had to be done. He and Bart saved quite a lot of money doing what they did, because both tasks were expensive to contract out.

George covered her mouth with her hand, and her complexion turned gray. "I really don't feel well."

Before Bob could blink, she turned and ran down the hall. The bathroom door slammed, and she started to retch.

Bob pushed the remainder of his burger into the center of the table. Suddenly he wasn't hungry anymore, either.

When everything became quiet in the bathroom, Bob walked down the hall and tapped softly on the door. "George? Are you okay now? Can I come in?"

The door didn't open. "I'm so sorry. Please go away."

Bob didn't go away. He couldn't remember the last time he'd been sick as an adult, but he clearly remembered his mother taking care of him when he'd had the flu as a child. Having someone who loved him care for him when he was down made the experience a little less horrible.

He seriously doubted George's father would have taken care of her. And while Josephine sounded like an efficient housekeeper, that's exactly what she was— paid help. For now, George didn't have the option of either one of them. The only one she had was him.

He wiggled the knob, and it turned. "At the count of ten, I'm coming in. Ten. Nine." Shuffling echoed from the other side of the door. "Eight. Seven." The doorknob moved, but since he was holding it firmly, he knew the lock button wouldn't work. A grumble came from the other side of the door.

"Six." He slowed his counting.

The toilet flushed.

"Five."

The water ran, and he could hear splashing and the frantic pumping of the soap dispenser, which reminded him that it was almost empty.

"Four."

"I give up. Come in. But you're not going to like what you see."

He opened the door.

George stood beside the sink, her arms crossed tightly over her chest, her shoulders hunched, and her eyes big and wide as she stared up at him.

"Are you okay?"

Her lower lip quivered. "No, I'm not okay. I don't think I've ever been less okay in my life." Her eyes welled up, and one tear spilled over onto her cheek. "I'm such a failure. I can't even do something simple like clean a bathroom without making myself sick. How pathetic is that?"

Bob stared at George. He pictured her as she had been on the day she walked in to apply for the job—poised and self-confident.

She wasn't like that now. Not only did she look defeated, she looked alone, and she was. Her father had abandoned her. He knew George had a sister, but she hadn't gone to her for help. As a tomboy, George probably didn't fit in with the other single women in her social circle, it hadn't appeared so at the banquet.

She really had no one to turn to besides him. The revelation was startling and heartbreaking. The expression *poor little rich girl* had never meant anything to Bob until now, and it put the verse, "What you do for the least of these, you also do for me" in perspective.

He'd given her shelter, but it was only his garage, which he wasn't even using. In a way, having her live there gave him the benefit of added security. No one would break into his storage area in the middle of the night with someone in the building.

He fully intended to buy her meals until payday, but that was as much for his benefit as for George's. Spending time together away from work when they went out for dinner together every Thursday night had made him realize how much he missed female companionship. George, unlike the other woman he'd dated, understood what he meant when he talked a little shop. He also could enjoy himself with no risk that anything more was going to happen than a pleasant evening. She knew his schedule and his obligations, and knew that the reason they were together was simply a weekly escape from routine. Thursday nights had become another routine, but one he enjoyed.

It suddenly hit him that they would no longer be enjoying Thursday dinners together. Up until now, George had insisted on paying every second time. Now, he refused to accept her money. She couldn't afford it, and he doubted she would accept more charity from him.

In a way, he was almost working on Tyler's manipulative scale. Bob was her boss. And a happy employee was a productive one. So helping George out ultimately helped him financially.

What George really needed right now was a friend who had nothing to gain by knowing her, and he couldn't make that claim. But he supposed that anyone else in his current position would probably give the poor girl a hug.

He started to step forward, but stopped. He didn't want to frighten her and he had her cornered in the small bathroom.

Bob remained in the doorway and extended his arms toward George. "Come here," he said softly.

Her lower lip quivered, and she came forward, but instead of throwing herself into him the way he expected a distraught woman would, she only leaned her forehead against the center of his chest. Fortunately, she didn't cry, which was good. If she had, he didn't know what he was supposed to do.

The only thing he could think of was to rest his hands on her shoulders, which he did. "Everything will be fine," he mumbled. "You just need to give yourself more time."

He felt her shake her head. "I don't know what I'm doing. Everything I do is wrong. And then when I think I'm doing something right, it backfires in my face. I can't even clean up without getting sick from the cleaner."

He massaged her shoulders with his thumbs. "That's just inexperience. You didn't know and you used too much. Next time, put only a little on the sponge, and you'll see that it goes a long way. You also picked the worst job first. I don't know why you didn't do the dusting and vacuuming before the bathroom."

"The bathroom was smaller, so it looked easier."

"Actually, it's not. Vacuuming is probably the easiest household chore."

"I don't know. I've never done it before."

Bob froze his movements. "You've never vacuumed?"

"Well, once. When I was a child, one day I thought

it would be fun to help Josephine, but Daddy saw me with the vacuum and took it away. He told me never to do that again, that I wasn't a housekeeper, I was an Ecklington. And of course, when I was a teenager, I grew out of wanting to help Josephine really quickly."

"Uh…do you at least make your own bed?"

"Of course not. But I wouldn't talk about not making the bed, if I were you."

A smile started to tug at the corner of Bob's mouth. The George he knew was back. "You'll do fine. You just need some help to get started. If you want, I can show you what to do."

He felt her nod again. "I'd really like that," she said, and as she spoke, she moved forward. Her hands fell to the sides of his waist, then started to inch to his back, but suddenly she stepped backward, covering her mouth with both hands. "I'm so disgusting!" she said between her fingers. "I have to go brush my teeth. One day, I'll pay you back for everything you're doing for me. I promise."

Before Bob could tell her that wasn't necessary, she squeezed between him and the door, and ran down the hall. The back door opened, closed and all was silent.

Chapter Eleven

Georgette slathered a layer of Bob's mother's home-made strawberry jam on her toast and took a big bite.

"Did you sleep okay last night? Most people don't sleep very well the first night in a new place."

She swallowed while she nodded, then sipped her coffee. "This is so delicious! Yes, I did. I slept great."

She'd truly slept like a log. Last night she'd wiped down the bathroom with water four times to get rid of the residue of pine cleaner, but this time, she went outside to clear out her lungs periodically. With the door open to air the place out, she'd vacuumed, dusted and even scrubbed out the insides of all the cupboards with dish soap.

At midnight, she dug through the boxes only long enough to find what she was going to wear to church that wouldn't need to be ironed, then dropped herself on the futon, more exhausted than she'd ever been in her life. She wasn't aware of a thing from that point on until Bob knocked on the door and told her it was time to get up for church.

Georgette checked her watch, knowing that they had to leave in a few minutes for Bob to be on time to practice with his friends before the service started.

She sipped her coffee quickly, enjoying common coffee as she never had in her life. More than feeling awkward in new surroundings when she woke up, she keenly felt the absence of a coffeemaker. And coffee filters. And coffee. And cream. And food.

The only thing she did have was a mug, but it was at work, which didn't do her any good.

There were so many things she needed, but the $3.37 in her wallet wasn't going to go very far.

She would have to pawn her expensive watch, even though she knew she would only get a fraction of its original price. The only other thing she owned of any value was the truck, and it would take too long to sell in its present condition. She could have money in her pocket from the watch Monday morning.

"Were you warm enough with that blanket I left for you? When we get back from church I'll give you some dishes and stuff out of my cupboard this afternoon, to get you started."

"I can't take your dishes."

Bob grinned. Georgette nearly choked on her current bite of her breakfast. The little crinkles that appeared at the sides of his eyes made him so attractive she stopped breathing. He always looked good in his customary attire of jeans and T-shirt, but today, dressed in black slacks and a neatly pressed blue cotton shirt for the more formal service, he was handsome in a different way.

"Sure you can. Technically, I really only need one plate, and so do you, if the dishes are washed and put away after every meal. I have a set of eight, so I can certainly spare a couple of sets of plates and cutlery. Besides, it's only a loan."

She didn't want to accept any more charity from him, but she was helpless not to. "Only if you're sure."

"I'm sure. Except you'll still be very limited as to what you can do. I only have one toaster, so if you like toast for breakfast, I'll give you a key for my house and you can come in after I leave in the morning. There are probably a number of other things you need that can't wait until payday on Friday, so I'm going to give you an advance on your paycheck."

"Are you sure?"

"Yes. I won't advance the whole thing, but I can give you a portion."

She looked again at her watch, which she now could keep, at least temporarily. "You have no idea how much I appreciate that."

"I know. Monday morning, pay yourself out three days. That should keep you going until Friday, when you can have the balance."

She finished the rest of the coffee in her mug, then set it down on the table, keeping her hands clasped around it. "I don't understand why you're being so nice to me. Not that I don't appreciate it, because I do. It's just that no one has ever treated me like this before." Not wanting to say so, she didn't understand his motives. Everyone always wanted something, and she was actually costing him money, with little or no chance of repayment, at least not for a very long time.

He shrugged his shoulders. "Do I need a reason? You need help, I have what you need and God put you in my path. I don't think it's any more complicated than that." He stood. "If you're finished, we really should go."

The drive to the church only took a few minutes, just as he'd said. There were only three other cars in the parking lot.

"It looks like Randy and Adrian beat me. Paul and Celeste aren't here yet."

"But there are three cars."

"That's Pastor Ron's car. He has to be here first to open up the building. Then he goes into his office to pray while everything is quiet, before everyone starts setting up for the service."

"Oh…" She'd never thought about what happened before a Sunday-morning service.

Georgette followed Bob onto the stage area. She stood to the side and watched as he started putting the drum set together. Adrian and Randy waved, then continued laying out cords and monitors.

"Is there something I can do?"

Adrian pointed to a carrying case beside the stairs. "You can assemble the microphone stands if you want. Everyone gets one except Bob.

She turned to Bob. "Why not?"

"I can't sing while I'm playing drums, nor would you want me to. I don't sing all that well."

Celeste arrived as Georgette finished assembling the last stand and Georgette went over to watch her set up the piano. "Have I told you how much I enjoy listening to you play? I took lessons for a year when I was a kid, but I wasn't very good. One day I took the keyboard off and was trying to figure out how the hammers were constructed and how everything worked together with the pedals, when my father discovered what I was doing and sent me to my room." Georgette grinned. "That was the end of piano lessons for me. They had to get a technician to put the piano back together, and he sold it a few days later."

Celeste smiled back. "The electric pianos aren't quite as interesting inside, but they are portable." She patted the corner of the unit.

Georgette turned to Randy. "Is there anything else I can do?"

"Nope. But I'm sure Pastor Ron would like some help setting up chairs."

Georgette gasped. "The pastor sets up chairs!?"

"Somebody's gotta do it—unless the congregation wants to stand or sit on the floor. That's the way it is in most organizations. Ten percent of the people do ninety percent of the work."

"Then I think I'll go set up chairs." She turned to Bob, who smiled his approval.

She expected Pastor Ron to be surprised at her offer, but he didn't refuse. However, when more people started arriving to help, the men took over and sent her away.

Since she no longer had anything to do, she stood to the side and watched the practice while the room started to take shape as a sanctuary. She'd never thought much about drums as an instrument, but watching the musicians go over selected parts until they got it right, she saw just how important it was for the drummer to give them the framework they needed.

When all the chairs were set up, she found a seat and waited for the service to begin.

It was very similar to the evening service, only more formal—except when the children were dismissed. They walked quietly out of the main sanctuary, but as soon as they crossed the threshold into the lobby, the running and screaming began, fading as the horde made their way downstairs to the classrooms.

Up on the stage, Paul smiled and shook his head, and the congregation sang one more song. As Pastor Ron started speaking, the worship team quietly left the stage, and shuffled into their seats; Bob sat beside her. Just as they did in the evening service, the worship team returned to the stage during the closing prayer so they could play the last song, and then the congregation was dismissed.

The instruments and equipment were left on the stage for the evening service so Georgette joined Bob on the stage, waiting beside him while the worship team picked up their music and put everything in order. Bob's cell phone rang, and he left the noise and walked to the back, where he spoke facing the wall for some privacy. The conversation was short, which Georgette was learning was typical of Bob. Within two minutes, he had returned.

"That was my mother," he said to the group in general. "I have to go to my parents' house for lunch. My mother wants to throw a big surprise party for my father's sixty-ninth birthday. I need to run over there for lunch, while he's out. My mother's called the family together to discuss the details, so I can't go out for lunch today." He turned to Georgette. "When I told her that you were with me, she invited you along too."

Georgette frowned. "A big party for his sixty-ninth? Why wouldn't she wait for a year and have something bigger for his seventieth?"

Bob grinned. "Because that's what Papa expects. Far be it from Mama to do what is expected of her."

Celeste remained straight-faced, but Adrian, Randy and Paul all grinned, as if they knew something she didn't. Georgette turned to Celeste.

Celeste shrugged her shoulders. "I've never met Bob's mom. But I will at the wedding. Oh, that's right, I nearly forgot. We need your address, Georgette."

"What? Why?"

Adrian slipped his arm around Celeste's waist. "Yes. We'd like to send you an invitation to the wedding, but I guess we can get your address from Bob."

Bob's movements froze. "Yeah. Or you can just give it to me when the time comes. You've got a few months still."

"I know," Adrian said, "but it's best to be prepared." He smiled down at Celeste. "I think we should get going so we can get a good table." He turned back to Bob. "See you tonight at the evening service."

Bob shifted into Park, and turned off the engine. The house blinds flickered when the car stopped, but he chose to ignore it. "This is it, my parents' house."

"This isn't far from your house, is it? Your house is about a mile and a half that way."

"Yes. Bart's parents live on the next block, and Bart and his wife Anna live two blocks that way. All close to work." He pointed to the left. "Our days are long enough without adding even more driving time."

He turned and put his hand on the door handle, but before he could open the door, George's hand on his other arm stopped him. "Why didn't you tell your friends that I've moved into your garage apartment? It was obvious they didn't know."

He released the door handle, and turned to her. "With those guys, I have to wait until the timing is right. I figured I'd tell them on Wednesday, at practice." Celeste wouldn't have thought anything special of it, but when he told the guys, especially Randy, he knew he would be in for the razzing of his life.

"Does your mother know?"

"George, no one knows. It all happened so quickly, and remember, I spent most of the day on Saturday at work, like I do every Saturday. It's just that I haven't had time." Not that he couldn't predict his mother's reaction. He had a woman living on his property. Regardless of the fact that George was living in a separate building across the entire yard, his mother would point out every possible and potential moral infraction imaginable. He knew he couldn't avoid the confrontation, however, so better sooner than later. He hoped his mother would at least lecture him in private, where George wouldn't witness it. After all, he was her boss, and he needed to maintain *some* dignity in front of her. "Let's go in. I saw the blinds move." For the second time since the car had stopped. "Just one more thing. Sometimes my family can be a little overwhelming, so don't take anything that happens too personally."

One eyebrow quirked, but George said nothing, so he led her up the walkway. The door opened the second his foot touched the first step.

"Hey, Rose! How's it going?" He turned to George as he stepped onto the porch near Rose. "This is my sister, Rose. Rose, this is George."

Rose's eyes widened, she blinked a few times and backed up to allow them to enter. "Hi," she said as they passed. "Mama is in the kitchen."

He took Rose's hint, and walked toward the kitchen. "Hi, Tony, Gene," he said to his two brothers, who were sitting on the couch in the living room, as he walked by.

"This is George. We have to talk to Mama. We'll be right back."

They smiled and waved without speaking, and George did the same. Bob slowed his pace and turned his head to speak to George over his shoulder. "I guess my other sisters aren't here yet. Gene's wife, Michelle, is probably in the kitchen with Mama."

In the background, Rose called Michelle, and as Bob and George stepped into the kitchen, Michelle passed them, nodding a greeting without stopping.

Bob's mother was stirring something on the stove.

"Hi, Mama."

His mother turned around, smiling. She looked up at Bob, her smile fell and her gaze lowered to rest on George, all five foot four of her.

"Roberto, you told me you were bringing your new mechanic, George. I think you need to get eyeglasses with your age. You have brought a woman."

"Mama, this *is* my new mechanic. Her name is George. George, this is my mama, Angelina Delanio."

George stepped forward. "Hello, Mrs. Delanio," she said smiling, as she extended one hand to his mother. Her voice dropped in pitch; she spoke evenly and in a friendly, conversational tone. Bob could see her years of fine upbringing being put to good use. "My name is really Georgette, but my friends call me George. I'd like to count you as a friend, so please, call me George. And I really am Bob's new mechanic."

His mother reached forward and slipped her hand into George's, but instead of a handshake, George covered his mother's hand with her other, gave it a gentle squeeze, and smiled.

Bob's mother returned George's smile. "Now I have

seen everything. But this is good my son has seen a woman can do such a job." Her eyes narrowed slightly. "You are doing a good job for him?"

George released his mother's hands, but the two woman remained facing each other, neither of them acknowledging Bob. He might as well have been invisible. "I like to think so," she said.

"He and Bartholomew started that business many years ago. My son, he works too many long hours. This must stop or he will drive himself to an early grave. It is good to see they have hired you."

Bob cleared his throat, wondering when he'd lost control. "Mama, there's something else. In addition to being my new mechanic, George is also my new tenant."

His mother's eyebrows knotted, and she planted her fists on her hips. "Tenant?"

"Yes. She moved into the garage apartment."

"For how long has this been going on?"

"George moved in yesterday."

Her eyes narrowed even more, and Bob nearly shivered with the ice in her glare, making him wish he were invisible. "How could you do a thing like that? It is so small. There is no room for clothes. And the kitchen! There is no kitchen! Jason could live on Antonio's pizza, but a woman needs a place to cook!"

"But…" Bob let his voice trail off. He'd thought all the same things, and he didn't have an answer. For George, the price was right, so that was all that mattered.

"Really, it's fine," George interjected. "In fact, I've never lived on my own before, so it's perfect. A small apartment is easier to keep clean."

"It is too small. Where are you going to put all your things?"

"I don't have very much. I actually have to go shopping tomorrow so I don't have to borrow so much from Bob. The garage apartment is just perfect for me."

"Well, if you are happy, then it is good to have someone new living there." She turned back to Bob "It has been a waste to have the apartment empty. Jason moved back home nearly a year ago. After all that work, and so much money you spent to fix it."

"I've been using it for storage. And you just said it was too small a few minutes ago. *"Mama! Mi fa la testa cosi!"*

She waved one hand in the air to dismiss his frustration. "Come, George. Come meet our family. Especially now that you are my son's tenant." She rested her hand on George's forearm and guided her back into the living room.

"Mama, I've already introduced them," Bob muttered, following behind.

His mother ignored him, and continued walking. When they arrived in the living room, he saw that his other sisters had shown up while he was in the kitchen. She stopped in front of the couch where Gene and Tony were sitting, and guided George to stand beside her. Bob shuffled to stand on George's other side while the introductions were repeated.

"George, this is my oldest son, Eugenio."

Bob leaned down to the height of George's ear, knowing his brothers could see what he was doing, but his mother could not. "Pst. He prefers 'Gene,'" Bob whispered, then straightened.

"And his wife, Michelle. Over here, this is Antonio."

Bob leaned to her ear again. "Pst. Tony."

"And his wife, Kathy. Here is one of my daughters, Rosabella."

"Rose."

"This is Maria."

"We couldn't shorten that one."

"This is my youngest child, Giovannetta."

"Gina," Bob whispered.

His mother leaned forward around George and glared up at Bob, obviously fully aware of what he'd been doing. "And of course you know my third son, Roberto," she said, rolling the *R*s, which she always did when she wanted to make a point or remind him of his heritage.

Bob stepped forward, grinned, pointedly cleared his throat and pounded his fist into his chest. "Me, Bob," he said, deepening his voice.

His mother picked up a section of the newspaper from the coffee table, and whacked him lightly on the head. "Respect your Mama. Your birth certificate, it says *Roberto*."

George grinned.

"Don't you dare take her side," Bob grumbled.

"Enough of this. It is time to eat."

Everyone filed into the kitchen and sat at the table while his mother and Rose set the food on the table. The room went silent while Gene said a short prayer over the food. At his closing *Amen,* everything erupted into the usual Delanio family get-together. At least three conversations were going on at the same time, with everyone involved in more than one. Rose and Tony started arguing about something Bob knew nothing about, and even Michelle started waving her arms in the air as she spoke to Gina about future party details.

Through it all, George was silent. She listened politely and responded when someone spoke to her, but she added nothing to the myriad conversations around her unless addressed directly. With friendly bickering, they agreed on enough details to begin planning the party.

After an hour, the timer on the oven began dinging.

"You must all go, except for Eugenio and Michelle. Your father will be returning soon with little Eddie after their fishing trip. He must not become suspicious. But we have a little time yet, George, would you like to come with me? I would like you to see some things."

"Of course, Mrs. Delanio."

Bob stood to accompany them, but his mother waved one hand in the air, halting him in his tracks. "Roberto, I need you to go to the garage and bring me four boxes. Hurry. Big boxes. Like this." She motioned the size with her hands, and he knew he was dismissed.

Bob sighed and went to the garage. His father regularly flattened boxes, *every* box they'd ever received, and stored them in the garage. For more years than he could remember, the entire neighborhood came to his mother when someone needed a box, and she always had just the right one, which of course, only made her worse.

By the time he returned, fifteen minutes later, he found a pile of miscellaneous household items piled at the back door.

"What's going on?"

"These things are for George. They are extra. I do not need them. Hurry and pack them into the boxes and carry them to your car before your father gets home."

"If this isn't going to be okay with Papa, then I think we should wait."

"Your papa will not even notice."

He scanned the pile. "This is a lot of stuff." But the more he thought about it, he thought that probably his father would be pleased to see it gone if he knew, as it lessened the volume of "valuable" things his mother stored in the basement.

"Hurry! Pack these things and go. Eugenio and Michelle are cleaning the mess in the kitchen, and I must help."

Before he could say anything more, his mother was gone. "I give up," he muttered.

Beside him, George giggled as she hurriedly began ramming things into the boxes. "I like your mother. I hope she manages to pull this birthday party off without your father finding out."

"If she doesn't, he'll still pretend to be surprised. He'd never do anything to hurt her feelings."

Bob picked up an old toaster he remembered using as a child. "I remember when this broke. Papa fixed it, but Mama had already bought a new one and used it, so she couldn't take it back. It's just like her to keep it all these years, just in case."

"Yes. She told me about that toaster. I'm just so stunned that she's given me all these things." She held up a towel. "Look at this! It's so soft! I can't believe she wasn't using it. She said she didn't like the color."

"Mama may seem pushy at times, but she has a good heart."

"Yes. She seems very sweet, and I love listening to her accent. Does your father have an accent, too? You don't."

"My parents immigrated right after they were married. In order to preserve the language, we always spoke Italian at home, and English when we were in school or out with others. We stopped speaking Italian as frequently when Gene married Michelle, because we didn't want to be rude when she couldn't understand us."

"So you speak Italian fluently?"

"Yes, but I don't use it as much as I used to."

"You said something in Italian when we were in the kitchen. What did you say?"

Bob blushed. "*Mi fa la testa cosi.* It's just an expression of frustration."

"But what does it mean? It sounded so regal."

"It's not. It means 'you're going to make my head explode.' Mama sometimes does that to me."

George started to laugh. The heat in Bob's face extended to his neck.

"That's so funny! What a way to put it."

"It's just an expression. You can't translate these things literally. Now come on, we have to hurry if you want to unpack and still have time to eat supper before we have to leave for the evening service."

Chapter Twelve

Georgette smiled broadly as she closed the cupboard door. All of the cooking utensils and supplementary things Bob's mother had given her were put away properly, including a few miscellaneous kitchen items whose purpose was still murky. The one thing she definitely knew how to use—a coffeemaker with a mismatched pot, was washed and sitting on the counter, ready for its first use—when she could finally buy some coffee.

Bob's mother had been so thorough that Georgette's remaining list of things to buy was now short and affordable. Exactly as promised, first thing that morning at work, Bob had given her an advance on her paycheck, which would be enough to buy the critical items on the list and enough groceries to last her until payday. She could still drive to work too, if that was the only place she went.

She even had a phone to use. Bob had given her one of the phones from his house, and pointed out a phone jack in the wall that was connected to his own line at his house. Not that anyone she knew would call her. Listening to Bob's private phone ringing felt odd to her, but he had wanted her to have a phone available in case of an emergency.

A knock sounded. Georgette grabbed her purse with a light heart. The only other time she'd felt so free was the day she got her job.

She opened the door and stepped outside. "I really appreciate you taking me shopping. I never really thought of how long your days are. You start before I do in the morning, then you close up more than an hour and a half after I'm gone. I see what your mother said about you working too much."

He sighed. "My mother means well, but sometimes she gets carried away."

Georgette tried to stop the wistful feeling that sneaked up on her. "Your mother seems like a wonderful person, and I'm sure she's only doing it because she loves you. I miss that."

Bob stopped walking. "I'm sorry, George, I didn't think. Don't get me wrong, I love Mama, and there isn't anything I wouldn't do for her. But when she has a point to make, nothing stops her from making it. I know I work too much. In fact, today Bart and I decided to cut back our hours. We're finally at a point where we're able to keep everything current. Starting tomorrow, I'll go home at the same time as you. Bart will arrive later, the same time as you, and he'll stay to close up at six. We even talked about each taking a day off midweek in addition to Sunday, because we both need to be here Saturdays; it's our busiest day. It hasn't been easy for us, but I think we can finally cut back to both of us working five days instead of six, and the business won't suffer."

Georgette smiled. In her own way, Bob's mother had

made her point and got what she wanted, which was the best for her children. One day, Georgette wanted to be that kind of mother, only she hoped she could make her point a little more delicately.

She looked up at Bob, whose face had softened while he thought of his mother. Before Georgette thought of being a mother, according to God's direction, a husband came first. She wondered what it would be like to be married to Bob. He was a considerate and generous man, a good son, and he would make a good father as well as a good husband. He respected his mother, regardless of her quirks.

Georgette shook her head. As much as she liked him, she could never forget that he was her boss—as he often reminded her.

Georgette forced her thoughts back to that working relationship. "What day do you think you'll take off?"

"Neither of us can take Monday because it's always really busy. Bart wants to be off Tuesday, so I'll take Thursday off. That way the shop won't be one person short two days in a row." He smiled and stared off into space. "It's been so long since I've taken more than one day off in a week. I've never even had a vacation in all the time we've been running the business."

Georgette couldn't imagine that. As busy as her father was, he always traveled twice a year, once in peak summer vacation season, and someplace exotic in February. "That sounds great. What do you think you're going to do?"

"I don't know. First I might catch up on a little sleep." He turned and grinned at her. "I certainly don't sleep in on Sunday morning. If I take Thursday off, I'll finally have some time to practice drums on my own during the daytime, when my neighbors aren't home. I think I might spend a little money and buy a spare drum set to keep at home. You have no idea how much work it is to lug a drum set back and forth every week between home, the church and Adrian's house. I don't want to move them any more than I have to."

"Or maybe you can buy one of those small electronic sets, with headphones to practice at home."

His grin widened. "Yeah. That's a great idea."

She wondered if one day, Bob's neighbors would thank her. The smile didn't leave Bob's face as he drove them to the big supermarket.

Once inside, she tried not to gape at the scope of the building. She stared up to the open ceiling and its metal rafters in which birds could nest without anyone being the wiser.

"George? What are you looking at? We should get moving. It's getting late."

She caught up with Bob, who was pushing one buggy for the two of them, since he only needed a couple of small items.

"How do you find what you need in a place like this?" The place had dozens of aisles that seemed to go on for miles.

One eyebrow quirked. "You learn the layout. I know where everything is, at least the things I buy. I guess this is bigger than what you're used to."

"You've got that right. We had groceries delivered."

Their first stop was the bakery aisle. She put a couple of loaves of bread in the buggy, along with a package of muffins that looked good, before she remembered that she had to make every purchase count.

She put the muffins back.

The next stop was the meat counter.

She stood, staring at the packages of…raw meat. Her stomach churned when she looked at a huge ugly mass labeled Beef Tongue.

"Not over there, George. Over here they sell single portions. It's a little more expensive per pound, but this way you don't waste anything and you don't have enough fridge space for more. Those pork chops look good." He picked up a package, and handed it to her. "What do you think?"

Georgette took in a few deep breaths to help force the picture of the mutilated cow parts out of her head, then turned the package over. "There aren't any directions."

"You don't need directions. It's just a plain pork chop. You fry it."

"Is that hard?"

Bob's mouth opened, but no sound came out.

"I don't think you understand. I've never done this before."

"You've never cooked a pork chop?"

"Not only have I never cooked a pork chop, I've never cooked anything. I've certainly never bought raw food."

Bob shook his head. "I don't understand. I've seen you bring some wonderful homemade things for lunch. Stroganoff. Chowders." His eyes brightened, and he smiled. "Lasagna. You even brought an extra piece for me. It was delicious."

"Josephine made all those things for me. She took care of all the meals and groceries. Besides, my father would never let me do anything so mundane as food shopping."

She held out the pork chop for him to put back. "I wouldn't be able to use this."

"Then what do you know how to cook?"

"I know how to make macaroni and cheese in the microwave."

Bob shook his head. "There's no room for a microwave in that apartment. You'd have to make your macaroni in a pot."

"You can make macaroni in a pot?"

Bob lowered his head and pinched the bridge of his nose. He mumbled something in Italian that she wasn't sure she wanted translated.

"I told you. If it's not something I've gotten at our deli or from Josephine, I don't know how to do it."

"You can make a sandwich, I hope? You know. Two pieces of bread, condiments, meat and maybe some lettuce and cheese?"

She couldn't tell if he was being sarcastic. All she knew was that people were starting to stare.

"Can we go someplace else to talk about this?"

He waved one hand in the air, the hand that held the packaged pork chop. "There is no place else to talk! This is the supermarket! Where people go to buy food! Which is what we're supposed to be doing!"

She lowered her voice. "You're shouting."

The volume of his voice lowered, but it was still tight. "What did you think you were going to buy here?"

"Besides the things on the list you said I had to buy, I need coffee. Maybe some cans of soup. I could probably do that without a microwave, too, couldn't I?"

"How did you think you were going to live on your own if you can't cook?"

"I never thought about it. No one really gave me the chance to learn, and now I don't have much choice. I'll figure it out." She extended her hand. "So give me back that pork chop."

Bob sighed, but instead of handing her the pork chop, he tossed it into the buggy, along with another one for himself. "I should have figured something was amiss when you didn't know what that chopping board my mother gave you was for. I can get you started with a few basic techniques. I certainly can't let you starve to death."

"Maybe cooking will turn out to be a hidden talent for me."

"Talented or not, you've got to eat. We'd better get moving. We have to get everything you need and be out of here before they close for the night."

Bob shuffled the bags he was carrying to balance on one arm, knocked on the door of the garage apartment, and waited.

He hadn't made it out the door at work as early as he'd hoped. Today he had promised George he would show her how to cook her own supper, which was supposed to be the pork chop they'd bought last night. With her questionable level of domestic ability, he feared for their safety if she were to start cooking without him.

The door opened.

"Sorry I'm so late, I…" Bob's voice trailed off as he looked at George's face. "You've been crying." He dumped everything he'd been carrying onto the futon, and grasped her hands. "Did you burn yourself? Are you okay?"

He turned and looked at the table, which was set for two. A pot and a frying pan were on the stove, empty and unused. It wasn't injury.

"What's wrong?" he asked, not releasing her.

"I've been thinking about my sister, Terri," she sniffled. "I tried to call her, but she wasn't home and now I can't stop thinking about her. I went to her house first when Daddy kicked me out, before I showed up at the shop. Her husband Byron was there, but he wouldn't let me in. I need to talk to her. Just in case I'm wrong. Or maybe just in case I'm right."

"I'm afraid I'm not following you."

George gulped. "I think another woman was there, that night and I want to talk to Terri about it, because if I'm right, this is something she should know. Everyone would tell me to mind my own business, probably her too, but I can't. I've picked up the phone a hundred times today. Then, when I finally got the nerve to finish dialing the number, Byron answered, and I hung up without saying anything. I'm such a coward." A tear rolled down her cheek.

Bob's gut clenched. He'd heard comments about watching a woman cry from his brothers and his friends. Joking aside, his stomach really did feel strange. He wanted to hold George and soothe away the tears, but he wasn't in a position to do that. Even though they were going to be spending a lot of time in each other's personal space while he helped her get back on her feet, he certainly didn't want to get in any deeper by getting involved with her family. The woman needed some privacy.

He ran his thumbs gently over the insides of her wrists, and she sniffled again. The lump in his stomach turned to a rock.

It might have made sense before, but his position made him feel like a hypocrite. His own family had pretty much adopted George in just one visit. After their lunch with his mother and siblings, Gene had called and asked if Bob was bringing her to his father's birthday party, since she'd already heard most of the preliminary plans. He only hung up for about ten seconds before his mother had called, offering to teach George how to make his favorite three-cheese lasagna. He didn't want to go there.

But he couldn't stand the thought of George facing her sister's marital problems without anyone to stand by her. With his large family, he'd never had to face a problem alone, unless he wanted to. He also had always had the support of his best friend Randy, as well as Paul and Adrian, and, of course, his partner, Bart.

Even though he'd lived by himself for over five years, Bob had never felt alone.

He didn't know what he could do, but if George tried to handle this herself, he felt as if he'd be sending her alone to face the wolves.

"Is there something I can do?"

"No. I don't even know if there's anything I can do." She cleared her throat. "I really think Byron is cheating on Terri, and I think she should be told. I don't even care if she hates me for saying something, which she probably will. But I can't say nothing. That's not the way God wanted marriage to be."

"Then I think you're right, you should talk to her."

"I want to, but I don't know what to say. Do I just knock on her door and say 'Hi, Terri, how's it going? By the way I think your husband is having an affair?' I don't know if I can do that. Besides, if I see Byron, I think I might just fall to pieces."

"I think you're stronger than that."

She said nothing. All she did was stare up at him.

He knew that her parents had separated when she was a child. Now with her sister's husband having an affair, Bob suspected that George had never seen the workings of a good marriage. On the other hand, Bob's parents had been wonderful examples. They were approaching their fortieth year together. When an issue came between them, they were often loud, but they always followed God's direction and worked it out.

One day, George would have someone to stand beside her, but for now, all she had was him.

"How about if I go with you?"

"Would you do that?"

"I wouldn't have asked if I didn't mean it."

"When?"

He turned to look at the pile of stuff he'd come with, strewn on the futon. He couldn't believe how much his life had changed in only a few days. He didn't want to deal with any more on an empty stomach. "After supper would probably be good."

She pulled her hands out of his, and swiped her eyes. "Of course. I'm so sorry. If it helps, I'm ready to start as soon as you are."

"For the first meal, I thought we could do something really simple and just fry the pork chops and have mashed potatoes. Let's start."

Bob showed her how to peel one potato, then he let her do the second one. He passed on his mother's instructions to use only enough water to barely cover any vegetable, including potatoes, and moved on to preparing the pork chops. He used the cooking spray he'd brought on the frying pan, and when the pork chops were sizzling, he spread on some of his barbecue sauce.

He showed her how to slice into the chops to see if they were done, then had George heat up a can of corn, and their supper was ready.

He knew his mother liked to put everything in separate bowls and set them on the table when serving more than one, but Bob only thought of having to wash more dishes. He placed the food directly and set the plates on the table.

"This is it. Let's eat."

George checked her wristwatch. "That took an awful long time for just one allegedly simple supper. Isn't there any way of doing it faster?"

"I'm afraid not. This is nothing. There are some things my mother cooks that take hours to prepare." He grinned as he thought of mealtimes when she served pasta asciutta, another family favorite. "Takes us only ten minutes to eat, though."

George planted her fists on her hips. "That doesn't seem worth it."

He shrugged his shoulders. "That's life. A person's gotta eat. Might as well make it good."

As hostess, George said the blessing. When she thanked God for his presence in her life, and then said what a blessing he'd been to her, Bob could barely choke out an answering "*Amen.*"

"Do you think I'll be able to do this by myself?" she asked after taking a few mouthfuls.

"I don't see why not."

"I guess I'll have to buy some sauce and stuff, won't I?"

He nodded. "Yes. But remember, that was only your first grocery shopping trip, only for the barest of basics. Next time, you'll have more money to spend."

They didn't rush but they finished quickly. Perhaps George had been as hungry as he was, but it was probably the errand looming over both of them, and without much more fussing around, they left to face Terri.

Chapter Thirteen

Bob followed George's directions to her sister's house, which was, as he had expected, in an area of the city where he could never afford to live. It made him embarrassed that his renovated garage was the best he could offer George, and his house wasn't much better than his garage.

He followed George to the door and stood to the side when she knocked. A woman who was unquestionably George's sister answered. Terri was taller than George, and her figure much more womanly, although he suspected her attributes were surgically enhanced. Still, George's blue eyes stared at him out of that heavily made-up face.

"Georgette? What are you doing here?" Terri glanced at Bob, then back to her sister.

"I need to talk to you. Is Byron home?"

Terri glanced to the street, then back to Bob. "No, but he shouldn't be too much longer."

"What I have to say won't take long. May we come in?"

"I suppose."

The second he was inside, Bob wanted to turn back and leave. White carpeting throughout, was the crowning glory of a pristine decor that shouted adults only. The uncomfortably sterile atmosphere also reminded him that he hadn't yet showered after a long day at the shop.

"To say I'm surprised to see you would be an understatement. Daddy told me that you ran away with some guy he didn't know. I'm assuming that's *you*." She spared Bob a rude glance before continuing. "He's been very upset. He told me that Tyler was going to ask you to marry him, but you left the banquet early, and when he got home all your things were gone. Where did you go? "Have you eloped? Daddy is very, very angry with you. You know how he's always wanted you to have a big wedding like mine."

Bob squirmed, not knowing if he should tell George's sister what had really happened, or if he should keep silent.

George stared down at the floor and cleared her throat. "No, I didn't elope, and that's not exactly the way it went. But I'm not here to talk about me. I'm here to talk about you."

Terri's eyes widened. "Me? Whatever for?"

"Terri, are you happy?"

She backed up a step. "Of course I'm happy."

"What about Byron?"

"Byron is fine."

"But does he love you? Do you love him?"

Terri stiffened. "I think maybe you should leave."

George shook her head. "I can't leave until I say what I came to tell you. Terri, I came here on Friday night, and you weren't home, but Byron was. I could be mistaken, but I think he had another woman here."

Terri's face paled. "You mean he had *her* here?"

George's face paled as well. "You mean you already knew?"

"Did anyone see her besides you? I told him not to bring her here."

Bob stood stunned, unable to believe what he was hearing.

"I don't understand. Aren't you going to do something about this?" Georgette asked her sister.

Terri blinked and stared George in the eye. "I'm going to tell him not to embarrass me, and to keep her away from our house."

Bob knew George's sister and brother-in-law weren't Christians, but that was no reason to accept infidelity in a marriage. He could no longer keep silent. "Excuse me, but are you going to counseling about this? There are things you can do."

She turned and stared at him. "This is none of your business. You two aren't even married."

Bob opened his mouth, but no sound came out. He wanted to say he was George's boss, but his reason for being there had nothing to do George's job. He was there because he wanted to help her and be there for her when she needed him. And that was wrong. He was supposed to be pulling back, not getting more entrenched in her personal life. George didn't need that complication and neither did he.

The most effective thing to say was that he was a friend, but he didn't want to go there. He couldn't cross that line.

"I'm Bob," he said, hoping he didn't have to clarify it with more, and felt George's fingers intertwining with his.

Terri stared down at their joined hands, and then

turned back to George. "Don't lecture me about right and wrong. I can't believe you ran away with someone Daddy didn't even know." She sniffed the air, telling Bob that what he suspected was true. Even though he always wore coveralls over his clothes all day, he still smelled like a grease pit. "Daddy doesn't approve of this at all."

"Daddy and I don't follow the same standards. He approves of things I would never do."

"And running off isn't wrong? What does your God say about what you did to Daddy?"

Since their arms were touching, he could feel more than hear George's quick intake of breath.

Bob gave her hand a gentle squeeze. He lowered his voice, trying to sound gentle, even though he could feel his anger building inside. "She didn't exactly run away. Your father kicked her out."

Terri stared at George, and backed up another step. "If Daddy kicked you out, then I don't want you here, either. And how dare you lecture me about what's right and wrong and all that religious nonsense, particularly with *him* here." She waved one hand in the air in Bob's direction.

Bob continued speaking, even though Terri wasn't looking at him. "We're not living together, and we're certainly not doing anything wrong. But we didn't come here to talk about us. We came to talk about you. You don't have to live like that. Fidelity in marriage is something everyone deserves. If you want, I can recommend a counselor."

Terri stepped around them, and opened the door. "I'm fine the way things are. It's time for you to leave. If you hurry and Byron doesn't see you, I won't tell Daddy you've been here."

"But..." George stammered.

"Get out."

Bob knew no progress would be made by arguing. It was time for Terri to mull over what they said. Maybe one day she would take him up on his offer of counseling, but that day wasn't today.

They left quietly, and not a word was said the entire drive home.

When Bob reached to turn off the motor he turned to George, but remained seated in the car. "You did your best. All you can do now is wait, pray for her, and hope she calls you."

"I know."

They left the car, and he walked George to the door of the garage apartment.

She unlocked the door, but instead of pushing it open, she turned to him. "Not that I didn't appreciate you going with me, because I know I would have fallen apart without you there, but I need to know why you came. Are you doing this because you feel sorry for me?"

Bob gazed into her wide eyes as he ran through a mental list of everything that had happened since he'd met George. Of course he felt bad that her family was rejecting her, but she'd acted honorably. He was proud of her for giving Terri that bad news. But he wasn't helping her because he felt sorry for her.

She was efficient and capable, and she just needed a little help to get over the hump. George always accomplished what she set out to do, even if it was the hard way. She'd earned the respect of his customers, and likewise, by her hard work and dedication, she'd also earned his respect.

Yet Bob wasn't at peace with what was happening

between them. He couldn't help it, but he sometimes felt twinges of jealousy because of the privileges she'd grown up with and taken for granted—things he would never know. Nothing had ever been out of her budget. She'd told him she had had all the latest and the greatest stuff, including a state-of-the-art computer and big-screen television, two things he really wanted but couldn't afford. She could have gone to the best university, if she had chosen her courses from her father's selected list. She'd always had the best clothes, any car in the world she wanted, and had lived in a home bigger than anything he could ever dream of with an indoor pool, sauna, and a private tennis court. She didn't merely play tennis, she'd taken private lessons on her own court.

The men she dated also had always known the same privileged life. Only in the last few years had Bob not had to worry about budgeting in the price of dinner and a movie if he wanted to take a woman out—if he could even take the time for a date from his work schedule.

Now, finally, he was able to work only five days a week. Still, he had to work, and he had to work hard in order to survive.

Until now, George hadn't had to work if she didn't want to. She could have lived a life of leisure, and it wouldn't have been wrong.

And now, all that was gone.

But as to her question, no, he didn't feel sorry for her. Still, he knew it wasn't smart to have gone with her, given what his presence with her implied to Terri especially when Georgette had grabbed his hand. She came from another world, a world where he was considered little more than the hired help. In hindsight, he supposed, her culture and refinement had been evident from the day he had hired her, in everything she said and did.

That a person like him could be the employer of a person like her was what he would have called one of life's cruel jokes. If the same thing had happened to someone else, Bob might even have considered it funny.

But Bob wasn't laughing.

Learning to make do with a modest income was something George had never had to do. For now, having to work and save money to get what she wanted, or even the necessities of daily life, was a novelty. Very soon, that would wear off and she would experience the frustration that came when sometimes, no matter how hard a person worked for something they wanted, the answer was still no.

He'd lived with a lot of no's in his life, and he knew how difficult it could be. He couldn't deal with the hurt and disappointment when he was unable to live up to her expectations. He certainly didn't want her to live down to his. Falling in love with someone from the other side of the tracks only worked in fairy tales.

"I don't feel sorry for you. You're my employee and you need help, so I'm here. I'll see you tomorrow, at work. Good night."

Georgette cut the last piece of meat, then picked up the cutting board to scrape the pieces into the pan in with a knife.

She shuddered as she picked up a slimy hunk that had fallen onto the counter, and tossed it in with the rest of the raw meat. "This is so disgusting," she muttered, then immediately went to the sink to wash her hands with the dish soap. The only thing that made her feel any better was the aroma of the meat frying as it started to cook.

"It's just stewing beef, George. It's the same as any other piece of beef."

She dried her hands on the dishtowel, then turned to Bob. "I didn't have to hack at the steak yesterday. I only had to make a few slices in it, pour that brown sauce on it, and let it sit."

He sighed, and she immediately felt ashamed of herself for her outburst. "We were marinating a less tender cut of meat. Today we have meat that needs more work. If you simmer it for a couple of hours, it will just melt in your mouth. Otherwise, it will be tough. These are things you have to do when you're living on a budget. You can't eat New York Cut steaks every day any more."

A wave of guilt washed through her. "I'm sorry. I know you're sacrificing your time to show me how to do this, and I really appreciate it. It's just that I never thought handling raw food would be like this. It's…" She shuddered again. "Not exactly pleasant."

Bob snickered and then his smile straightened with a visible effort, although Georgette could still see the corners of his mouth twitching. "Maybe tomorrow I should show you how to stuff and roast a chicken. There's nothing to cut when you roast a chicken."

He spoke with a straight face, but his lower lip wouldn't stop quivering.

Georgette narrowed one eye. "Is that hard?"

"No."

"Is there a catch?"

"Maybe."

Both eyes narrowed. "What?"

"You don't have to do anything from the outside, but

when you buy a chicken, there's a bag inside the cavity, you know, the hollow part where the guts were."

Her stomach churned. "I'm not sure I understand. Why would there be a bag?"

"They save the heart and liver, and put them in a bag, and put the bag in the cavity. You have to take it out before you cook the chicken."

If she didn't feel sick enough thinking about it before, the queasy sensation quadrupled at the thought of reaching inside a disemboweled animal and touching the internal organs. "If they're in a bag, then I don't have to look. I don't have to reach inside, do I? Can't I just shake the chicken, and everything will drop right into the garbage can and I don't have to watch?"

"You don't want to waste it. Mama cooks the liver and chops it up then she adds bread, onions, celery and spices to make the best stuffing you've ever tasted in your life."

Georgette held back her comments and turned her attention to the small counter and the table, both strewn with dishes and utensils. A pile of potatoes and vegetables lay on the counter, which she would cut up and throw in later, after the meat had cooked for a while. "I had no idea this was going to be so much work, and look at the mess already! Do you go through all this every day, when you're cooking for yourself?"

Bob pressed both palms over his stomach, which was quite tight and flat, and grinned. "I love to eat, so unless I go home to Mama every day, that means I have to cook. But I will tell you a secret. When I make a chicken, I do exactly just what you were saying. I throw the innards out, and use the instant stuffing you buy in a box and make it in a pot. I don't mind cooking, but usually I don't make anything fancy and I like to have leftovers. Now, my brother, Tony, he loves to cook even more than he loves to eat. He can cook as good as Mama, even better on some things. But don't ever tell her I said that."

"Tony owns and operates a restaurant, doesn't he?"

"Yes. God has really blessed our family. Tony loves to work with food as much as I love to work with motors. We've each managed to run a business doing what we love the most. God really opened the doors for both of us."

Georgette wasn't sure she agreed. Over time, she'd seen how hard Bob worked, and she knew the long hours he put in. He also hadn't always run a good profit margin. God had certainly made it possible, but He hadn't made it easy.

She didn't understand why men like her father had it easy, when good men like Bob didn't. Her grandfather had passed the chain of stores on to her father, so her father didn't have to put his heart and soul into building the business; it was already very successful when he took over. That hadn't stopped him from doing many things she considered questionable, if not downright unethical to increase his profits.

Bob, on the other hand, sometimes barely broke even in a transaction, simply because he honored his estimates, even if the situation wasn't in his favor.

Lately she'd been finding that when she came home from work, she missed him, especially now that she had reminders of him everywhere. She heard the minute he came home, because he parked his car on the cement pad next to the garage. Today, she had stopped what she was doing and listened to him as he cut the engine and walked past the garage to get to his house.

Her heart pounded sharply until he showed up back at her door, ready to demonstrate the meal of the day.

It was foolishness. He had been more than obvious in his professional feelings, yet she couldn't help but compare Bob favorably to every other man she'd ever known. Despite the privations of his youth, Bob was satisfied with his life. He was who he was, and that was a nice, honest man who put God and his family first in his life. It made him easy to love, and one day, when he decided to settle down and get married, he would make a good husband to a very fortunate woman.

A twinge of jealousy for a woman who didn't exist yet flashed through Georgette's mind.

Bob walked to the fridge, opened it, and began rummaging through the meager contents. "Now is the time for you to put in an onion. I know we bought some."

She couldn't help but watch him. Bob was physically fit because he worked hard all day, but she didn't often see him without his baggy coveralls. Up until now, his coking lessons had kept her running around too much to notice, but at this moment she had nothing else to do but watch.

Georgette blinked, and forced herself to get her mind back on cooking, and away from how good Bob looked, especially from the back. "I think they're on the second shelf, behind the yogurt."

He reached in further, then backed up, an onion in his hand. "You're supposed to put the onions in the bin marked for vegetables."

"But I didn't want the carrots to smell like onions."

"Don't worry, that won't happen. Although, you should have kept the onions in the bag."

"Really? But they weren't in a bag in the store, so I

thought you weren't supposed to keep them in the bag at home."

He shook his head. "Nope. It's best left in the bag. Now it's time to cut it up and put it in with the meat as it cooks."

She accepted the onion, and searched in the drawer for her one and only chef's knife, which had been given to her by Bob's mother. "Is it true what they say about onions, that they make you cry? I've never dealt with one raw."

"Then you're in for a bit of an education, George."

She had received more education in the last three days than she'd had in the last three years, but Georgette held her tongue.

He stepped closer when she placed the onion on the cutting board. "There are a number of old wives' tales about cutting an onion, but I think it's just best to do it quickly. First cut the ends off, peel it and then cut it up into bite-sized pieces."

Georgette did as instructed, and soon she had half the onion cut. At first, the strong smell was just annoying, but the more she cut, the worse it became, and soon, her eyes were burning and watering.

She looked up at Bob and smiled. "I see what everyone means."

"You'd better stop talking and hurry up. I don't want to end up like you!" As if to emphasize his point, he chuckled and stepped back.

"Coward," she sniffled. "This isn't so bad. It burns, but I can take it." Except that her nose was getting increasingly stuffed-up, and her eyes were overflowing. She cut a little more, and the burn worsened, making her want to close her eyes, which she couldn't do if she was going to finish cutting up the onion. The tears became more irritating as they dribbled down her cheeks.

She sniffled again, and raised one hand to swipe away the tears.

"No! George! Don't wipe your eyes with your…"

Using the back of her hand, she rubbed over her left eye. "…hands…"

"Ow! Ow!" The sensation changed from a burn to a stab of pain. Her eyes squeezed shut of their own accord, and she dropped the knife to raise her hands, but stopped them in midair, trying to overcome the urge to rub her eyes. "I can't see! It hurts!"

A warmth enclosed both wrists. "Come to the sink. Quickly."

She followed Bob as he dragged her to the sink. He enclosed both wrists with one hand, and the water started running. She heard splashing, and he pulled both her hands under the water. "Bend down so your face is over the sink. Keep your hands under the water." He released her wrists, and one wet hand pressed into the back of her head. A gush of warm water splashed over her eyes, followed by another. "Try to open your eyes now."

She managed to open both, but the left eye wouldn't open more than a slit.

"Keep them open."

Before she could respond, a couple more splashes of water hit her.

"That helped," she sputtered, spitting out some water that had splashed into her mouth before she straightened.

"Good. Now wash your hands with dish soap, and you'll be able to finish what you were doing."

She dribbled some soap onto her hands, rinsed them and returned to the chopping board with the half-processed onion. Working quickly, she swiped the cut pieces into the pot and swiped the remainder of the onion into the garbage. "Forget it. That's enough. I don't need so much onion anyway."

"That's cheating."

"Too bad," she muttered as she ran water over the chopping board and knife, standing back as far as she could while doing so. When the board was sufficiently rinsed, she knew she should turn around, but she didn't want to. Without looking, she knew her eyes were red and puffy, her face was streaked and blotchy, and she would have unsightly splashes of water down the front of her T-shirt.

She'd never looked so bad in her life, not even on the day her father had kicked her out of the house.

It shouldn't have mattered, but she'd already lost everything; all she had left was her appearance, as silly as that might seem. The harshness of her new reality smacked her between the eyes. How ridiculous to be brought so low by a lowly onion, but there it was. She stood before Bob rejected by her family, homeless and ugly.

She didn't understand why everything was happening to her this way. She hadn't led a bad life, even before she became a Christian, yet God allowed everything to be stripped painfully away.

She turned around, only because she couldn't keep her back to him all night.

Bob lifted his wrist and checked his watch. "I think you have everything under control now. I have to go, I'm already late for practice. Cut up the carrots and celery and throw them in, then in an hour, cut up the potatoes and add them, too. When the potatoes are cooked, you'll have made your very first batch of beef stew."

"But there's so much here. Will you be back in time to help me eat it?"

"Sorry. Worship team practice won't be over in time. I'm going to grab something quick on the way to Adrian's. We were supposed to start early tonight because Paul has to be at the school afterwards for some kind of competition." He began walking to the door, hesitated, then turned around. "I feel so strange. I almost said that I have to get up early in the morning, too, but I don't." He grinned from ear to ear. "I get to sleep in."

"I hope the noise of my truck starting in the morning won't wake you up."

"Don't worry, it won't. By the way, when I was talking to Adrian earlier today he said he's going to have some time to stop by and go over the books with you tomorrow, to get a start on what he needs for our corporate taxes. I think you'll be fine without me, so I told him it was okay." He checked his watch again. "You'll have enough leftovers here to last you through supper tomorrow, so I guess I'll just see you Friday at work. Bye."

Chapter Fourteen

Bob missed his timing with the cymbal, then hit the lower tom harder than he should have. Completely losing the beat, he paused, intending to listen to everyone else and regain his bearings. Instead, without him keeping tempo, the music ground to a slow and painful halt.

Paul shifted his bass guitar so he wouldn't hit Adrian with it as he turned, and stepped toward Bob. "Is something wrong? You've been having trouble keeping it together all night."

"Nothing's wrong," Bob muttered. "I just have a lot on my mind."

Adrian turned around to face him. "I hope it doesn't have anything to do with tomorrow. If you're not ready, I can do it another day."

Bob shook his head. "It's not that. In fact, I'm not even going to be there. George has been doing a really good job. The bookkeeping is as ready as it's ever going to be."

"You mean you won't be there? Where are you going to be?"

"I don't know yet."

All of his friends turned and stared at him.

Randy left the sound board, walked right up to him, and stared him in the face, not breaking eye contact as he spoke. "You mean you're taking a day off? Midweek? And you don't have specific plans? Is everything okay?"

Bob cleared his throat. "Things have never been better. That's one of the reasons Bart and I hired George in the first place, so that we could work only five days like everybody else. Now that we're finally at that point, I have to admit I don't even know what I'm going to do with myself. What do you guys do when you have a day off?"

Adrian shrugged his shoulders. "I've never taken one off midweek. But if I did, I'd probably go to the library and get a new book to read. I'd practice learning something new on my guitar, too, probably."

Randy grinned. "I'd go shopping."

Bob turned to his best friend. "Are you nuts? You work at the mall. Don't you see enough of it during the week?"

"That's different. I don't get enough time to do real shopping. Maybe instead I'd go online and play games with whoever else is on at the time."

Bob shook his head. "Computer games," he muttered. "Don't you think you're getting a little old for that? You really are crazy. What about you, Celeste?"

"I'd probably do the same as Adrian. Read. Practice my piano for a while. Play some of my favorite songs. Work on some new ones. Stuff like that."

"What about you, Paul?"

"I don't get days off one at a time. When the kids aren't in school, we have workshops and seminars to keep current with what's going on. If I were to have a few days together, like in the summer, I would go somewhere I've never been. See the sights."

Bob nodded. "Well, maybe I can come up with something. Let's finish up practicing these last couple of songs before it gets too late."

"This is great, much better than I expected," Adrian said to George. "Bob's transactions are usually so disorganized it takes me weeks to sort through them. You've got it all balanced, and it's reconciled, too."

George smiled up at him. "Thanks. I've worked hard to get it to this point. I finally got them to give me a written record of every transaction, including what they buy online. It's much easier to enter everything and balance it when I can follow a paper trail."

Adrian nodded. The last time he'd balanced Bob's books had been the worst. He hadn't been looking forward to it at all this time, but George had surprised him. "They really needed a professional bookkeeper. You've done a great job."

"Thanks. I do my best."

While George typed in the command to call up a journal of the payroll taxes that were due to be paid the next day, Adrian looked through the window into the shop, where Bart was working, all alone. "It's so strange to be here, and not see Bob."

"I know. But it's been something we've all been striving for."

"Yeah. Last night he was trying to think of what to do today. Do you have any idea what he decided?"

George shook her head, and hit the key to print the screen. "No. Last I talked to him, his only goal was to sleep in. I made sure I was really quiet when I left this morning, so I wouldn't wake him."

Adrian nearly dropped his pen onto the floor. "Wake him?" he sputtered.

"Yes. He's always gone before me. In fact, it's been kind of my cue to get up. He's like clockwork. I don't even need my alarm clock. I just get up and start getting ready when Bob starts his car. It was just so strange today, trying to be quiet because I knew he wanted to sleep in, particularly since I really need to fix my muffler."

"Let's back up. What's going on?"

She sighed. "New things like the muffler keep coming up all the time—I just don't know where the money will come from. I know I need a new one, but Bob is teaching me how to prioritize my expenses. We figure if I let it warm up for only a minute, then the noise shouldn't annoy his neighbors too much. By the time the muffler blows completely, I should have saved enough money to fix it." She turned and grinned at him. "Bob said I only have to pay the wholesale cost on the parts, and I can do the work myself in the shop after hours, which will save me a lot of money. I should be able to get it done in a couple of weeks."

"I'm still not getting this. Annoy Bob's neighbors?"

"Yes. The muffler noise is annoying to any of the neighbors with windows open, or thin walls, for that matter."

Adrian stared at George, at a loss for words. Last night everyone had noticed Bob's strange behavior. They had all assumed Bob was obsessing about taking time off, and Adrian had thought it quite amusing, as did the others. Everyone had had their little laugh, brushed it off and moved on.

Apparently, they'd been wrong. There had been more going on than any of them could ever have guessed.

George walked to the printer and pulled out the printed sheet. "It sure is different than what I'm used to, actually depending on an older vehicle for transportation, rather than just playing around and fixing it up as a hobby."

Adrian raised his palms in the air. "You'll have to forgive my bluntness, but have you, uh…" Adrian stammered, trying to think of how to say what he wanted without sounding like he was making an accusation, when actually, he was.

He shook his head. "Forget it. I'll just come right out and ask. Have you moved in with him?"

George's face paled, which Adrian wasn't sure was a good sign. He didn't know her well enough to know if she was shocked by what he'd asked or by being caught.

"You mean he didn't tell everyone at practice last night?"

"Tell everyone what?"

George sighed. "I've been having some troubles with my family. I needed a place to stay, so Bob is letting me live in his garage apartment."

"Garage apartment?" Adrian crossed his arms over his chest while he gathered his thoughts. "Oh, that's right. That's where his cousin stayed. Are you saying that you've moved into Bob's garage?"

Her cheeks darkened. "It's really quite a nice apartment. It's a little small, but the longer I'm there, the more I like it."

Adrian narrowed one eye while he studied George. Randy had cornered him after Paul, Bob and Celeste left. He had insisted that something was going on between Bob and his new mechanic. Adrian had brushed it off at the time, but it seemed as though, for once, one of Randy's crazy hunches was right. In hindsight, Bob really had been far too distracted to be thinking only about taking a simple day off work. If George had been having family problems, it was just like Bob to be concerned and try to figure out a solution.

George looked down to the floor. "Adrian, you've been friends with Bob for years, haven't you?"

He nodded. "Yes. We grew up together. All four of us have."

"So you know him pretty well, then?"

"Yes, I like to think so."

"He told me on Sunday he was going to tell everyone at practice that I had moved into his garage apartment. Yet now, I find out he didn't. Do you think he didn't say anything because he regrets letting me stay there?"

"No, I don't think so at all. Bob wouldn't have made such an offer if he didn't mean it. But he kept zoning out on us all night, and now I know why. Bob works best when he can focus on one thing at a time and he's obviously got a lot to think about. That's how he built that business from nothing. One step at a time. It's just the way Bob is. Bob doesn't multitask. Randy, now there's a man who multitasks." Adrian shook his head.

"Pardon?"

He turned back to George. "None of us can figure out how Bob and Randy can be in the same room together sometimes. Randy can't function unless he's doing fifteen things at once. Bob grabs one thing at a time and worries at it like a dog with a bone, before moving on to the next thing. Yet they've been inseparable since we were kids."

"I don't think I know what you're trying to say."

"I'm not sure I can explain it. Bob is a very linear thinker. He's got to have something all figured out before he can talk about it. So while something *is* bothering him, it's probably not exactly you living in his garage. It's more." Adrian paused to think of Randy's suspicions. Randy had it figured out, but the more Adrian thought about it, the more he also thought that Bob hadn't figured it out yet.

Adrian bit back a grin. In the future, he'd have to give Randy more credit.

"Don't tell anyone I said this, *especially* not Bob, but I think he likes you. I'm not the only one who thinks that, either. He likes you so much it's distracting him."

It was awhile before George finally spoke. "I don't think it's that. Bob is teaching me to cook, and he's helping me learn how to manage a budget and balance my checkbook. He's so good at showing me what to do, and how to do it. He's so patient, no matter how many mistakes I make."

"Remember Bob is the youngest boy in his family, so he knows what it's like to be the underdog. At the same time, his sisters are all younger and he helped care for them when they were little. Bob's got the ultimate middle-child syndrome."

George's eyes widened, but she didn't say anything.

The more Adrian thought about it, the more he could see why Bob was having difficulty making everything fit together. He would have to deal with George one way at work, and another way on their shared property.

Again, it would be a different set of rules when he was in her home, or when she was in his.

"Do you have any advice for me?"

"I'm afraid I don't. All I know is what it was like for me, before Celeste and I were engaged. There were things I wish I'd known sooner, but I guess it all worked out. I like to be prepared, but life doesn't always work that way."

Georgette smiled. "See, there's some advice for me, after all."

Chapter Fifteen

"Bye, Bart!" Georgette called out. "See you tomorrow!"

"Bye, George!"

The entire trip home in her truck, Adrian's words echoed through Georgette's head. *I think he likes you.*

She couldn't help it, but she liked Bob too. Yet just as Bob needed time to think about what was happening, so did she. Above all, she had to be realistic. Bob was her boss, her landlord, her tutor, and recently he'd become somewhat of a spiritual mentor. She didn't want to think that he was acting like a big brother just because he had three younger sisters.

As she turned into Bob's back lane, she saw the garage door was open, displaying the storage area Bob had built. Bob, wearing coveralls, stood on the pad, next to something she'd never seen him with before.

A big, big motorcycle.

Georgette drove up, parked her truck and approached Bob. "What in the world is that?"

"It's my baby. Isn't she a beauty?"

Georgette ran one hand over the chrome handlebars.

She didn't know much about motorcycles, but she could tell it was old. "What year?"

"She's a 1949 Harley-Davidson Series F Hydra-Glide Solo, a real classic. It was the first year they introduced the hydraulic front forks." He paused to run his hands down the chrome plating of one of the forks. "She used to belong to my father, but he wasn't really interested in motorcycles, so he gave her to me when I got old enough to drive one responsibly. Of course, I had to get her running first."

"If he wasn't interested in motorcycles, what was he doing with it?"

"Someone gave it to him. A friend didn't have any money to pay for some work Papa did, so he bartered the motorcycle instead. It wasn't in very good condition, but Papa felt obligated to take it."

Georgette had a feeling that Bob had learned many of his kind ways from his father, whether they were good business practices or not. "It looks like you've done a good job fixing it up."

He ran one hand lovingly over the leather seat. "Thanks. It took me a long time to get her to look like this. I thought today would be a good day to take her out—with all the work I've been doing, I haven't been able to lately."

A slow grin began to spread on his face. "Do you want to go for a ride when I'm done?"

Georgette's heart pounded so hard, she thought Bob would be able to see the movement through her T-shirt. For years, it had been her secret fantasy to ride a motorcycle, but she didn't know anyone who owned one, nor did she have a motorcycle license.

She hugged her purse as she studied Bob's bike.

The burgundy paint shone in the sunlight, and when she moved, the reflection of the sun off the polished chrome nearly blinded her. The motorcycle was big and proud, it would be noisy, and it would turn heads. The force of the wind would be exhilarating in the rush of the speed.

She steeled herself. "Have you got an extra helmet?"

"Of course." He pointed to two helmets, exactly the same color as the bike on one of the shelves in his storage area.

Her voice quivered as she spoke, and she couldn't stop it. "Need some help getting it in shape to go?"

He bent down, picked up a wrench and handed it to her. "Here you go."

They worked in silence for a few minutes, but it didn't take long before Georgette couldn't stand it anymore. "I didn't know you had a motorcycle. Why didn't you tell me?"

He shrugged his shoulders. "There isn't much to tell. I own a motorcycle. So what?"

"I haven't seen it or even known about it in all the time I've known you."

"It's a noisy thing to start up early in the morning, so I can't take her to work. Like I said, I had a few things to fix up before I put her on the road again. I belong to a Christian motorcycle group, and it's our annual camping trip soon, so I need to get her in good shape."

"Camping trip?"

"Yeah. Usually we head up into the mountains, but this year so many people are going, we rented a couple of acres on a ranch. We head up Saturday, have a big barbecue together for supper, and camp out Saturday night. Sunday we have a worship time and short service, then have a big picnic to finish up the leftovers before everyone goes home."

"You like doing that?"

Bob nodded. "Yeah. We go in groups of twenty or thirty bikes, and we all meet there. There's nothing like being in the middle of a bike caravan. This year I think they're expecting five hundred people."

"Where do they put everyone? Where do you sleep?"

"I told you, George. It's camping. Everyone brings a tent and a sleeping bag and one change of clothes. There's not a lot of room to carry stuff on a motorcycle."

"A tent? You mean you sleep—" George gulped "—on the ground?"

"Yup. That's what camping means. Sleeping on the ground in the great outdoors. Haven't you ever gone camping before?"

She shuddered just thinking about lying on the ground with the bugs and whatever else was down there. "No."

He sighed. "I forgot. You've probably traveled around to all the great cities of the world, where you only stay in the best hotels. You've probably never not had running water."

Georgette pressed one hand over her heart. "No running water? Where do you...uh..."

Bob sighed again. "The people who do the organizing rent chemical toilets that don't need flushing."

"Ew."

"It's not as bad as you think. It's actually a nice break to get away from a busy life. We sing songs by the light of the moon, under the starry sky. You can't see the scope of the heavens or the number of stars under the city lights. I think you'd really be amazed. If you came, I bet you'd enjoy yourself."

"But I don't have a motorcycle. I've never even been on one before."

"Lots of couples come, and not everyone has their own bike. A motorcycle seats two."

"But you and I… We're not…you know."

He shrugged his shoulders. "It's a Christian campout, George. Not every couple that comes is married. It's well-chaperoned, and at night, it's divided into three sections. One for families and married couples, one for the single men, and one for the single women. And let me tell you, the single men *far* outnumber the single women. You've still got lots of time to decide. It's not this coming weekend, it's next weekend."

"That's only ten days away."

"Like I said. Lots of time."

"What about the shop?"

"I do this once a year, and Bart runs things by himself for a day."

George stared at Bob. She wanted to think he'd invited her because he cared for her in a special way, but Bob's deliberate reference to the abundant supply of single men contradicted that. Still, it was something she'd never done. "Let me think about it."

"Sure. We're done. Are you ready to go?"

She studied the bike. Suddenly, instead of looking like fun, it felt intimidating, now that she was so close to it. "I don't know."

"We can make your first ride a short one. How about if we just go to the grocery store, and come back with something to cook for supper."

She looked down at the saddlebags attached over the rear tire. They were as small as Bob said, but they would certainly hold enough for one meal.

"Okay. Let's go."

He handed her a helmet, then helped her fasten the chin strap so it was positioned securely. Satisfied, he closed the garage door and locked it, put on his own helmet, then slid onto the motorcycle. "Come on, George. Hop on." He patted the seat behind him.

Suddenly her doubts pressed in on her like a wall.

The motorcycle didn't have a seatbelt. The only way to stay on and not fall off was to hold something, and that something would be Bob.

But now that she had the helmet on, it was too late to change her mind.

"Don't be nervous. I'm a safe driver, and I'll take the corners carefully. All you have to do is hold on tight, and lean with me. I haven't dumped it in five years."

"Dumped it?"

"That's when something happens and you lose your balance and the bike lands on its side. With a bike this size and weight, it takes two men to get it upright again. That only has to happen once, and it's a lesson learned for life. It's really embarrassing." He patted the seat again. "Up you go."

Inhaling deeply, Georgette walked stiffly to the motorcycle and slid on behind Bob.

The seat was surprisingly soft. For a short trip, it would be fine, but she couldn't imagine sitting on it for hours and still being able to walk with any sort of dignity afterward.

Beneath her, the motorcycle roared to life.

She stiffened from head to toe.

Bob twisted around to look at her. "This is it. Hang on."

When he turned so he was once again facing forward, she gently rested her hands on the sides of his waist.

He twisted slightly, flipped the visor up once more, and looked into her eyes. "Not like that. You'll never be comfortable enough to enjoy the ride if you're not holding on properly. Like this."

Before she could think of what he was doing, his hands pulled hers forward and pressed her palms onto his stomach. The unexpected movement sent her front into Bob's back, her head landing between his shoulder blades.

He patted her hands, then let go. "Just remember to lean with me."

Without waiting for her response, he took off.

Georgette squeezed her eyes shut and hung on for dear life. She pressed herself into Bob's back, and didn't move. When they came to the first corner, it took every piece of strength within her to lean into the curve with him, feeling the pavement approach the tender flesh of her leg.

Bob slowed as they approached a red light, and she could feel his body shift as he extended one leg to support the bike while they waited for it to turn green.

Georgette opened one eye. Nothing seemed abnormal as they sat in the traffic. She opened the other just as Bob revved the motor, which she took as the cue that they would be moving in another second or two.

From behind him, she watched as the world went by in a glorious rush.

She didn't feel entirely safe being so open to the elements, but she was starting to feel more comfortable.

Not moving her hands from the security of Bob's stomach, she straightened her back so she could see better. Riding on the back of the motorcycle was fun. Kind of like the scariest ride at the fair.

Too soon, Bob turned into the supermarket parking lot.

She slid off the bike first, then Bob followed. He engaged the kickstand, pulled off his helmet, and smiled down at her. "Did you enjoy the ride?"

She pulled off her own helmet. "Yes! I can hardly wait for the ride home."

"First, we have to buy something to make for supper."

"What do I do with this?" She held out the helmet.

"I'm afraid we have to carry them. I don't have a lock to keep them on the bike and if we don't take them inside, someone will steal them. Sad but true."

She followed Bob inside and through the store, selecting some vegetables and a package of chicken fillets. The ride home was much more enjoyable than the ride to the store, and when they pulled onto the pad beside the garage, Georgette was sorry it was over so soon. The only reason she didn't ask Bob to keep going was that she was so hungry.

"What are we making today?"

"A stir-fry. Only because I'm really hungry, I'll cut up the chicken, and leave you to cut up the vegetables, so we can get it done faster."

She remembered the disgusting process of cutting the beef. She didn't imagine cutting raw chicken was any different. "You won't get any argument from me on that one."

When they were done, she followed Bob to the stove. "First you put a little oil into the pan, let it heat up a bit, and before you add the chicken you test the heat. Mama showed me how to do this. Splash a few drops of water in the pan. If the water rolls in a little ball for a second before it evaporates, the oil is ready."

With Bob standing and watching, she did exactly as

he said, and strangely, the drops of water did stay in a little ball rather than a puddle when he splashed some in. Bob tossed in the chicken, stirring and showed her what to look for to tell when it was time to add the vegetables.

Leaving Georgette in charge of the stir-fry, Bob began rummaging through her fridge.

"Don't you have any soy sauce?"

"No. We haven't ordered Chinese food because I didn't have enough money."

Bob stood. "Soy sauce doesn't only come in those little packets, you can buy it in a bottle. I have some at home. I'll be right back. Just remember to stir this in a couple of minutes, so it doesn't burn."

"Will do."

Instead of staying by the stove, she walked over to the window to watch Bob as he dug his keys out of his pocket and went into his house. She pictured him walking to his kitchen, since she now knew the layout. The phone rang, causing Georgette to flinch and breaking her reverie. So she returned to the stove and stirred the cooking chicken, as instructed.

She waited for a minute, then gave it another stir. A watched pot might never boil, but a watched stir-fry was making her restless.

Georgette walked to the television and flipped it on to listen to the news. Then it was time for another stir, so she walked back to the stove, tended to their dinner, and went back to the television where the theme had changed from world news to local, and a reporter came on with a live broadcast of a boat accident under one of the city bridges that had tied up rush-hour traffic when the boat hit one of the bridge supports.

Just as a city engineer started describing the steps it

would take to ascertain that no permanent damage was done, Georgette smelled smoke.

She ran back to the pan, which had started smoking. Time seemed—slow. Just as she reached for the spoon to stir everything again, the smoke alarm in the center of the room began to screech. Her hand continued its course and the exact second she touched the spoon, the contents of the pan burst into flame.

Time snapped back into focus. Georgette backed up, unable to believe what was happening. She ran to the cupboard, grabbed a glass, then ran to the sink to fill the glass with water. She had just filled the glass and aimed it at the flames, when the door burst open.

"What are you doing?!" Bob exclaimed as he ran for the stove. He grabbed the lid for the pot and threw it on top of the flames. It landed crooked, but he made a quick jab at it to push it so it fit squarely. He blew on his fingers, turned off the heat, then stuck his fingers in his mouth.

"How did this happen?" he yelled around his fingers. "I thought I told you to stay there and stir it every couple of minutes." He pulled his fingers out of his mouth, looked at the reddened tips, then shook his hand in the air.

Georgette couldn't answer, not that it would have made any difference. The screeching of the smoke alarm would have drowned out anything she said.

Bob reached forward and pushed the button to turn the fan above the stove on, then ran some water over his fingers in the sink. After a few seconds, he muttered something else under his breath, dragged a chair under the smoke alarm and took out the battery.

The only sound remaining was whirring of the fan above the stove.

It was still too silent.

Bob returned to the stove, and using a towel, he lifted the lid to confirm that the fire had been extinguished. "It's out," he grumbled.

Georgette felt her lower lip quivering, but she refused to cry. After everything that had happened, and after everything she'd done, she didn't want to give in to the last sign of weakness and defeat.

"I'm so sorry," she mumbled. Her eyes burned, but she blinked a few times to fight it back. If she said any more, she knew she would lose control, so she remained quiet.

Bob waved one hand in the direction of the stove. A black smear marred the stove hood, and a cloud of smoke hovered next to the ceiling over the space of the entire apartment. "How could you let this happen? I told you not to leave it."

She stiffened and tried to be brave, but her voice came out in a squeak. "You didn't exactly say that. You told me to stir it in a couple of minutes. When I heard the phone ring, I knew you'd be gone longer, so I actually stirred it a few more times."

His arm dropped to his side. "And what were you doing with a glass of water? You of all people should know better. That was a grease fire. It was the oil that was flaming, not the meat. Water spreads a grease fire."

"There isn't a fire extinguisher here, so I didn't know what else to do. It didn't occur to me to smother it."

The sound of canned laughter drifted from the corner of the apartment that was officially the living room.

Bob's eyebrows knotted, and his eyes narrowed. "Were you watching television?"

"I got bored, and then I got distracted. I'm so sorry." She bit into her lower lip, to keep it still.

Bob ran one hand down his face. "No, I'm the one who should be sorry. I should have come straight back. I also shouldn't have yelled at you."

Georgette stared at Bob, waiting, although she didn't know exactly what it was she wanted. It felt like a moment from a TV commercial, where Bob would open his arms, welcoming her. Then, in slow motion, she would glide across the room into them and they would close around her. His kiss would make it all better, and end their first fight.

Bob sighed, disturbing her thoughts. "I guess we'd better clean up, and decide what else we can make for supper. I have a fan that I can put it in the door to see if we can get more air circulating to clear out the smoke."

Without waiting for her to comment, which would have been pointless anyway, he turned and walked out, leaving her all alone.

The stove fan continued to whir, reminding her of how stupid she'd been.

She'd failed again.

Georgette looked at the charred meat inside the pot, and swept her hand over the top to check the temperature. It was still warm, so she set it aside to cool completely before she threw it out.

Her father had been right when he said she could never live on her own. She couldn't even cook an edible meal by herself.

Rather than do nothing, she retrieved the pine cleaner and a sponge, two things she had come to know quite well, and began scrubbing the black spot, standing on a chair to reach. She didn't even bother to turn around when clunking behind her signified Bob's return.

The noise level increased significantly when the second fan started.

"If you're interested, we can eat the leftover stew from yesterday," she said as she wrung out the sponge. "I think there's enough for both of us."

"No, I think I'll leave that for you for tomorrow night, because I'm not going to be here. I'm going out with Randy." He paused for a few seconds. "You do know how to heat something up without a microwave, don't you?"

She dipped the sponge in the water again, and resumed scrubbing. "I've never done it before, but I'm sure it's not difficult."

The pause before he spoke was almost tangible. "Tell you what. Tomorrow at lunch time, I'll go out and make an extra house key for you, and you can use my microwave. It's probably a good idea for you to have a key for my house, anyway."

Georgette felt herself sinking to an aptitude level below that of the common earthworm.

She kept scrubbing, not trusting herself to speak.

"For today, I have a solution for supper." Bob picked up the phone and dialed. "Hey, Tony. It's me. Bob. Can you send over a house special pizza to my garage?" Bob paused. "Yes, I said the garage, very funny. Jason used to order pizza all the time. Thanks."

Georgette felt herself sinking lower, if that was possible. Even Bob's brother knew how hopeless she was.

Her father was right. She would never survive. Even her boss's family knew it. Unless she could live on peanut butter sandwiches. *Those* she could make without setting anything on fire or doing anything else potentially fatal. Of course, she could always cut off her fingers in the process.

"George? I don't think you're going to get that any cleaner. Pretty soon you're going to take the paint off."

She froze, staring at the stove hood. Bob was right. No black remained. The surface was back to its original luster.

She turned around and smiled weakly. "This pine cleaner and I, we have a history together."

Bob approached her, standing in front of her as she remained standing on the chair. It felt strange to look down at him. She'd never seen the top of his head before. His hair was dark, thick and slightly wavy. She wanted to run her fingers through it, to see if it was as coarse as it looked.

He tipped his head up and trapped her with his vivid olive-green eyes, eyes that were the only criteria for that dress she'd purchased, a dress she would keep for the rest of her life, simply because of those eyes.

"It's okay, George. Everyone makes mistakes. You're still learning. I just keep forgetting how little you've done before."

"It's not okay. I can't do anything right. The only thing I can do without some disaster happening is my job. Someone has to do everything else for me, or I mess it up."

"That's just inexperience, not lack of ability. There's a big difference. You have loads of ability. It's just… never been tested."

"That's not true. Every time I do a test drive on my abilities, something needs to go back for repairs."

She glared down at him, daring him to differ.

"Will you get down from there? I can't talk to you like that."

Before she could refuse, his hands circled her waist, and he lifted her down from the chair.

Her heart pounded in her chest. Don't let go. Don't let go, she chanted inwardly.

His hands remained fixed on her waist. "I've never seen you make the same mistake twice, so that means you're learning, and you're teachable. That's the first thing I thought when I hired you. You were anxious and willing to learn, and sometimes that's almost as important as ability."

She went to raise her free hand almost as if in a dream, but discovered the hard way that it was too confining to rest her hand on his shoulder, which had been her intention. Rather than let her hand drop, she positioned her palm on his chest, over his heart.

She opened her mouth to tell him that his kind words meant a lot to her, but no sound came out. His body heat warmed her hand, and his heart beat accelerated beneath her palm. All coherent thought deserted her.

His grip on her waist tightened slightly as he drew he closer. One eyebrow quirked as he looked down at her.

She couldn't help herself, she let her eyes drift shut and tipped up her chin.

His lips brushed hers in the lightest of kisses. Not wanting to let the moment end, Georgette leaned forward, just enough to increase the contact slightly, to savor the softness of his gentle kiss.

She felt a soft sigh escape from Bob under her palm. His hands drifted slightly so they were more to her back, and his mouth came fully into contact with hers.

The sponge dropped from her hand.

Bob's kiss deepened, and he kissed her in a way she'd never been kissed before, as if he meant it.

Fool that she was, she kissed him back in equal measure.

A gentle rapping came from the doorway. "Bob? I got your pizza."

In a split second, Bob stepped back, breaking all contact. A shiver of cold coursed through her at the loss.

"That shouldn't have happened. I have to go. Keep the pizza. I'll see you at work tomorrow."

He stumbled around the fan, past the boy with the pizza in his hand, and was gone.

Chapter Sixteen

"I am an idiot," Bob muttered to himself as he reached up to the muffler of the car on the hoist above him and pulled on the tail pipe.

He picked up his hammer and began to hit at the muffler to loosen it, when out of the corner of his eye, he saw George through the window, dealing with a customer. She was as efficient as always. Polite. Cheerful. Proficient. Capable. Soft. Warm. A great kisser.

Bob took a harder swing at the muffler and missed shattering the exhaust pipe mounting bolts instead. The pipe itself hit the frame, then bounced back, narrowly missing his head.

"I'm a *total* idiot," he grumbled as he yanked it off, then stomped to the parts area for a new one.

"You're talking to yourself again," Bart said as Bob walked by.

"Ma fatti affari tuoi," he grumbled.

Before he could walk two more steps, Bart was beside him.

"I remember what that means, and you're wrong. It

is my business when you walk around talking to yourself. What's going on with you and George? And don't try to deny it. She's been acting funny today, too."

Bob sighed. "I lost it last night, and things went further than I wanted them to go."

Bart stiffened. Bob had never seen Bart's eyes open so wide.

"Don't look at me like that," Bob muttered. "Her honor is fully intact."

"Then what's the problem?"

Bob waved one hand in the air toward her. "She's our employee, for crying out loud! What would happen if we got personally involved?"

"I dunno. The business would turn into a three-way partnership?"

"Not funny, Bart."

"I wasn't trying to be funny. I really like George, but if you're doing something that's going to cause her to stumble…"

Bob swiped one hand down his face. "It's not that at all. It's just that she's got too much going on in her life to start something, even if she wasn't our employee. The fact that I personally hired her makes it even worse."

"I know she's got a few things to deal with. Everybody does. That's life."

Bob made a mental list of all the things that had gone wrong in George's life in the past few weeks, from Tyler to the situation with her father and then her sister, to her complete lack of experience in looking after her own daily needs, for starters. "You don't know the half of it," he mumbled.

And yet, as much as he knew it wasn't wise to get involved, he still wanted to help her be the person God wanted her to be. It wasn't likely God meant that to include kissing her.

"Earth to Bob. Hello, Bob. Put the landing gear down."

"Sorry. I was thinking about something. What did you say?"

"I said, I think you two should go out for coffee and talk, and get things back to normal. If that's not possible, at least make some kind of agreement that will allow things to go on the way they were before around here. I'll hold down the fort while you're both gone."

"No, that won't be necessary. I actually don't have much to say. It might even be a good idea to do it now, before the rush starts. Can you watch the front?"

Bart nodded and followed him into the lobby.

"George, I think we need to talk. Let's go into the office. Bart's going to run interference for us."

Her face paled. "Uh, sure…"

The second the door closed behind her, she spoke, her voice coming out barely above a squeak. "Am I fired?"

"No, of course not. But if you're worried about that, then it *is* best that we talk." He sat behind the desk and clasped his hands together on the desktop in front of him, trying to get himself into "boss mode" when he really felt more like a teenager.

When she was seated, Bob cleared his throat. "First of all, I need to apologize for yesterday."

Her face paled even further. "Apologize? But—"

Bob held up one hand to silence her. "Please. I'm finding this really difficult, so I'll just come right out and say it. I'm not sure what's happening between us, but what comes first is that I'm your boss, and I can't do anything to jeopardize that relationship. I've heard and seen too many times when people who work together start dating, and then the relationship ends. There are only three of us here, and we work together too closely to risk that kind of thing, so I think it's best to stop right now, before things get out of control. I think we can stay friends, and if we both keep that in mind, I think we'll be fine."

"Are you still going to show me how to cook and help me figure out a budget and all that stuff?"

"Of course. I said I would, and I have no intention of breaking a promise."

Her eyes widened. Bob felt as if he'd been poleaxed. He'd never seen a woman with eyes like George's. She sat before him, dressed as unwomanly as possible in her coveralls and safety workboots, complete with a streak of grease across her left cheek. Yet he'd been fighting the urge to gently wipe the smudge off ever since she'd come into the office. He knew that if he touched her, everything he was trying so hard to do would be lost in an instant.

Even though he'd been fighting his feelings toward her all day, now that they were together, her eyes held him like a deer in the headlights. He couldn't look away. Sincerity, hope, innocence and trust, all shone through right at him. He knew the difficult turns her life had taken. He wanted to move mountains for her, and it hurt him deep inside to know he was just a mechanic.

"What about next weekend? The campout with all your biker friends. Am I still invited? I was thinking about it all night, and I really want to go."

Bob's breath caught in his throat. The campout was his one break in the year—for two short days, his motorcycle took him to a place where no one could reach him, and he couldn't reach anyone else. This year, the organizers had encouraged everyone to leave their cell phones at home, or keep them turned off and pretend they wouldn't work on the wide-open ranchland the same as in the mountains, which blocked the signals. This was where Bob could retreat into rest and quiet, put all his problems and worries in a box for the weekend and listen to God talk.

Except he'd already promised George she could go with him.

But then, the quiet retreat would probably be good for her, too. It would be selfish if he didn't let her go.

"Of course you're still invited," he said, forcing himself to smile. He reached into his pocket. "Before I forget, I went out on my lunch break and made this key for you, like I said I would. Feel free to go in and use the microwave any time you want."

"I don't want to intrude. When will you be home?"

"Not until late. I'm going to the mall as soon as I get off, to meet Randy. As soon as he gets off, we're going shopping."

"Shopping? What are you going to buy?"

Bob's grin reached from ear to ear. "He's going to help me buy an electronic drum set. I can hardly wait."

Bob steered his motorcycle into the row of other motorcycles, and cut the engine. Supporting the weight of the bike with his leg until he could get off and engage the kickstand, he pulled the helmet off his head and turned around, still seated. "Here we are, George. It's time to dismount."

George pulled off her helmet, but remained on the bike. "I don't think I can move."

He grinned. "You'll only be stiff for a few seconds, and then you'll be right as rain."

"What a stupid saying. Who made that up, anyway? When it rains, I don't feel very 'right.' All I feel is cold and wet."

"There's only one way to get limber and that's to quit stalling. Just do it."

Before she had a chance to attempt to get her joints working again, a voice came from Bob's right side. "Hey, Bob! Good to see you."

He turned. "Hey, Brad. Good to see you, too."

Brad turned to George and smiled at her. "Care to introduce me to your friend?"

Bob squirmed invisibly on his seat. The entire trip, he'd been telling himself that it would be a good thing for George to meet eligible men, nonetheless, what he kept *feeling* were her arms around him as she rode behind. Now that he had someone to whom he could introduce her, Bob wanted to punch him in the nose.

He eked out a smile. "George, this is Brad. He's a wimp. His bike is one of those foreign makes."

Brad grinned. "Yeah. My bike actually lets people hear each other talking when they ride. I can demonstrate if you want to come for a ride with me."

"I'm sorry, I'm not sure I can get off *this* motorcycle, never mind get on another one."

"Some guys get all the luck," Brad said. "When you decide that he's not your type, have Bob give you my phone number."

Her face turned ten shades of red. "Uh…yeah… sure…"

At her reply, Brad moved on in the direction of the barbecue, from which Bob detected the aroma of roasting hot dogs. He mentally kicked himself for not being sorry to see Brad leave.

Finally, George slid off the seat, allowing Bob to slide off as well. He engaged the kickstand, and turned to George.

"What did you think of the ride?"

She rubbed her backside, obviously not caring if anyone around them was watching. "It was fun until it was time to move. How does anyone sit on those things for so long?"

"I guess we get used to it. Are you hungry? They have the barbecue going already."

"Yeah…" She inhaled deeply, grinning as her voice trailed off. "I sure am."

"Don't get too excited. It's just hot dogs. They have to keep the costs down."

"No, you don't understand. Daddy never barbecued anything, certainly not hot dogs, and neither did Josephine. I once had a hot dog from a vendor, but it was pretty gross, to say the least."

He supposed hot dogs, like meat loaf, for example lacked upper-class appeal. His family, on the other hand, loved meat loaf, even though it wasn't on a typical Italian menu. And when they all got together in the summer time, they always had barbecued hot dogs because his father could put more of them on the barbecue at once than anything else.

He led her to the barbecue, where she ate two hot dogs, loaded with onions, mustard and ketchup, then gave him half of the third one when she couldn't finish it.

He noticed a few raised eyebrows, and he did feel strange eating the rest of her hot dog—it spoke of a closeness that they didn't have. People seemed to move beyond that, though and during the course of the day, he introduced Georgette to as many people as he could, men and women. The group varied in age and background, but she connected with them all.

He helped her with the small dome tent he'd brought for her, and they set it up together in the area designated for the single women. She merely stood back and watched as he set up his own tent in the area for single men, as he claimed it wouldn't be good for his male ego if she helped him.

By the time the sun had set, about five hundred people had arrived, as expected. A number of campfires had been started, and about a dozen people with guitars scattered themselves throughout the site, all wearing battery-operated headsets so they could hear the leader and play the same thing at the same time.

"They're going to start in a few minutes. This is going to be really fantastic." Bob spread out a blanket over the grass, and they sat.

"Why aren't you playing something with them?"

"I play drums, not guitar."

"Drums aren't electric. At least not your old ones. You could play them here."

He grinned. "A drum set doesn't easily fit on the back of a motorcycle."

"Oops. I never thought of that."

The strumming guitars halted their conversation, and soon the rich sound of five hundred voices carried songs of praise throughout their own gathering, echoing off into the distance to whatever animals lived on the land.

Bob preferred a small congregation to a large one, but the combined effect of so many people singing and worshiping together was like nothing else, especially outside, where there were no boundaries. He wondered if this was a small sampling of what it would have been like during the journey of the twelve tribes of Israel in the desert, except those people would have been walking, not arriving on motorcycles of course.

Though George didn't know all the songs, unlike him, she participated where she could, and a few times he thought he saw tears shimmering in her eyes.

At the end of the worship time, everyone broke into small groups to pray, to catch up on events since the last time they saw each other, or simply to spend time with a friend.

As more people crawled into their tents for the night, Bob eventually found himself alone with George. He led her away from the brightness of the fire and pointed to the sky. "Look at the stars. You don't see this from the city."

She tipped her head up. "I've never seen anything like it. It's breathtaking."

"This time of year you see more shooting stars. They're fascinating to watch. This is the only time I can forget about everything and just be quiet in God's presence. Looking up at the big, wide-open sky reminds of how little I really am, and how big God is. Big enough for all our burdens."

George sighed. "I have to admit that I've never had so much to deal with as I have in the last few months. But when I'm busy all day, and so tired at night, I can push it aside. Here, though, I feel like God is telling me to make some decisions."

He turned and looked down at her. At work, and even in the kitchen with one notable exception, he didn't stand particularly close to her. Yet now, in the quiet of the dark, open field, with nothing and no one else nearby, her small size made him want to get as close as he could, wrap his arms around her, and shelter her from the world.

Instead, he picked up one hand, linked her fingers in his, and gave a gentle squeeze. "Then this is probably a good time to be quiet, pray and let God speak. Care to join me?"

"Yes, I'd like that."

He regretted the loss, but he had to release her hand to flip open the blanket he'd been carrying, and spread it on the ground.

He sat, and patted the blanket beside him in invitation. Once she was sitting, he lay flat on his back to look up at the night sky, his hands linked behind his head in contentment.

"This is the best way to see everything. Don't be shy."

"You know I'm not shy," she said as she flopped down on her back and assumed an identical position.

They lay in silence, looking up. Bob tried not to let her proximity distract him from God's leading. He turned his thoughts to how to pray.

Things were going well for his business, Bart was enjoying fatherhood, and in one short week, Adrian and Celeste were getting married. All in his own life was good. George, however, needed a lot of help and even more prayer.

He cleared his throat and tried to sound casual, but his insides churned. "Is there anything you'd like me to pray about for you?" As if he didn't pray for her every day already.

"I don't know. I think things have been pretty good. I have a good job, a nice place to stay. I'm making new friends." Even though Bob remained with his head facing straight up, he sensed George turning to look at him as she continued. "I have you helping me with everything. I thank God for you and all you've done for me every day."

Fortunately, the dark night hid his blush. "Thanks," he mumbled.

"I'm learning so much, I think it won't be long before I'll be able to manage on my own. So really, everything is good except for two things." She sighed, and her voice lowered in pitch to barely above a whisper. "Daddy, and my sister."

He hated himself for asking, but he had to know. "What about Tyler?"

"I've thought a lot about him. I still think that the way it played out was his fault, but I have to be realistic. Daddy would have found out what I was doing sooner or later. I can't say anything would have happened any differently if I told him instead of Tyler. I've been doing a lot of reading on forgiveness. If I don't forgive those who wrong me, it doesn't hurt them. It hurts me and my relationship with God. I've got to let it go. It's past, there's nothing I can do, so I have to move on."

As much as everything George said made sense, Bob didn't know if he would have been as gracious in the same situation. His own family accepted him unconditionally, of course, if he did something they didn't approve of, he heard about it for months. But still they forgave him, just as God forgave him for past wrongs and even future ones. The unqualified forgiveness made him eager to please God.

"That's great. I'm glad you can think of it in that way."

"There's actually a little more. Tyler was just being true to his own nature, which is to do anything to get ahead. It's simply the way he is, and I've always known that about him. He didn't even mean it personally—I was just a means to an end. He'll have to answer for that one day, but I can't judge him. That's not up to me. It's up to God to judge."

"Wow. I'm impressed."

She made a short, humorless laugh. "Don't be. There's so much junk on television that I've been doing a lot of reading. Celeste loaned me a few books, and what I was talking about came from one of them. That doesn't mean I have everything worked out. I haven't been able to fully forgive my father. I knew I was spoiled, but Daddy didn't give me everything because he loved me. He used it all to control me. And I let him because I was too much of a wimp."

This time Bob couldn't remain still. He rolled onto his side, and propped his head up with his arm, resting his elbow on the ground. "You're certainly not a wimp. You took the job knowing your father wouldn't approve. You went to church and worshiped God knowing he wouldn't approve. Then when push came to shove, you didn't cave in, but sacrificed everything you knew and took on a world of unknowns rather than do something you knew wasn't right."

She rolled onto her side and also propped her head up. "That's not exactly true. I knew you."

Bob opened his mouth, but no words came out. Not wanting to look too stupid, he rolled onto his back again.

He heard the movement as George also rolled onto her back. "I know it's something I have to work out, and I know I have to keep praying about that. But I really would like it if right now we could pray for Terri. I've phoned her a few times over the past few weeks, and she wouldn't talk to me. But yesterday when I phoned, she finally eased up a little and we talked. I think she'd been crying. She said that even though she wasn't happy with Byron, at least she could do what she wanted, which was more than she could do when she was living back at home. She won't do anything about Byron, because she doesn't want to have to go back. I tried to tell her that God would help her if she would only let Him, but she hung up on me again."

"That's so sad. It's easy for us to say, but you're right. She really could do something about it if she wanted to. I think it all comes down to how much a person is willing to sacrifice in order to do what they feel is right."

Thinking of George's sister, who preferred to remain miserable in order to keep her privileged lifestyle, emphasized for Bob how much George had given up to be free.

He liked to think that if the same thing happened to him, he would be able to do what George had done, but he'd never had to face something so hard. All his life, Bob had lived with very distinct guidelines of right and wrong. He'd never known a time when God wasn't acknowledged and obeyed in their home. As an adult, he lived the same way his parents had raised him, which was to try to love other people as God loved them, warts and all.

He knew he was a sucker for the underdog, but George wasn't an underdog at all. Despite her struggles, she was emerging victorious. Very soon she wouldn't need him any more, and they would go back to the way things had been before, whether she lived in his garage or not. He supposed her indomitability was one of the reasons he'd fallen in love with her so quickly.

Love.

Bob squeezed his eyes shut. All this time, he'd refused to consider that his feelings toward George were anything other than sheer altruism, but he'd been fooling himself. He did love her. He didn't know when it had started, but that didn't make it any less real.

What also was a reality was that he could never provide the things she was used to. For now, scrubbing toilets and cooking onions was a new experience, even a novelty. Very soon, it would become drudgery. She would become bored, feel trapped and resentful of having to do those things.

While the partnership in the auto shop with Bart was successful enough, neither of them would ever be rich. Up until now he'd been perfectly content. His life plan was to have a wife and children and raise his family the same way he had been raised, although Bob had no intention of having six children. Four would be good enough.

But George had grown up with an army of staff—a nanny, a housekeeper, gardeners, chauffeurs—so she didn't have to lift a finger, if she didn't want to. He couldn't see George being happy slaving over a hot stove while children tugged at her legs to go outside to play ball and the laundry piled up, and then he came home tired and dirty after a hard day at work and fell asleep on the couch.

He knew she would say it didn't matter, and maybe it wouldn't for the short term. But Bob needed someone who could be content in that atmosphere for a lifetime.

When George's warm hand rested on top of his, Bob sucked in a deep breath and tried to rein in his thoughts.

"Can we pray now?"

"Sure."

He led with a few words of praise to start, but their prayers drifted off to silence as they prayed individually, their hands still joined. Bob's prayers were mixed between concerns for George's sister, her father, for George herself, and even for Tyler. In praying for himself, all he could do was ask for guidance and promise to be open to God's leading.

He was startled when George pulled her hand out of his and sat up. "I don't think anyone else is awake except for us," she whispered. "We should probably get to our tents."

He sat up, and sure enough, everything in the huge expanse of the campsite was dark. "Yes. Tomorrow we're going to have another morning worship time, finish up all the leftovers for lunch, and then everyone will head home."

"I have a feeling tomorrow is going to go fast."

"Yup. Before we know it, we'll be back at work on Monday."

Using the flashlight sparingly, he led George to her tent, then went quietly to his.

Monday was going to come much too quickly.

Chapter Seventeen

"Hi, George. I see the counter's full. Where would you like today's mail?"

Georgette hit Enter on the keyboard, and stuck out her hand. "I'll take it…"

As the mail carrier left out the main door, Bob walked in from the shop door. "I'm expecting a letter about some warranty work. Is it in there?"

Georgette picked through the pile of envelopes, but stopped before she made it all the way through the pile.

"What's wrong? Is there something that isn't for us?"

"No. There's something here with my name on it. Something marked Personal and Confidential." Her heart nearly stopped when she recognized the company name on the return address. "This is from Tyler." She grasped the envelope by the corner, and immediately marched to the shredder in the corner.

Bob appeared beside her and snatched the envelope from her hand just as the corner touched the mechanism to activate it.

"Wait. Aren't you going to look at it?"

"No."

"What if it's something important? If you want to shred it after you've read it, fine, but you should see what it says."

She almost started to argue, but her words caught in her throat. No one knew where she lived. Even if they had, Bob's garage didn't have a separate street address. She didn't have a phone listing that could be traced through directory assistance. She'd tried to give Bob's phone number to Terri, but Terri wouldn't even write it down.

Her only tie to her former life was that Tyler knew where she worked.

If something had gone wrong or if her father or her sister were sick, no one had any way of contacting her except through Tyler.

"Maybe you're right." She accepted the envelope, opened it and began to read.

Dear Georgette,

I'm sorry to be sending this to you at work, but I couldn't find any other way to contact you. I want to tell you how deeply I regret what happened. Before you feed this through the shredder, I want you to know that I think about you every day, and wish we could start over under different circumstances.

Unfortunately, I can only beg you to speak to me. I would like it if you would meet me for dinner one evening soon. I know I will never be able to make up to you for what I've done, but please let me try.

Your father doesn't know I'm sending you this message, and quite frankly, I no longer care. I now understand your conviction to follow your own path, and your own heart. If your father fires me for attempting to contact you, then so be it. There are other jobs and other corporations, but there is only one Georgette Ecklington, and I miss her.

Fondly, Tyler

Georgette's hand shook as she tucked the paper back into the envelope.

"What's wrong? Is it bad news?"

She shook her head. "Tyler says he misses me, and he wants to get together and talk."

Bob's face turned strangely pale. "Are you going to?"

She ran her fingers over the envelope and skimmed through the letter once more. Despite Tyler's lovely words, she wasn't sure if she could trust him. He'd hurt her badly, and his actions had changed her life forever. The Bible told her to forgive Tyler, which she had, but the Bible didn't tell her to let him do the same thing to her a second time. But if he was sincere, and if things did go well, a union between them would see her gain back everything she had lost, without the roadblocks her father had set before her.

If he was sincere. It was a big *if*. The only way to know would be to see him in person and hope she could be discerning enough to tell the difference.

She looked up at Bob to see that he'd been watching her.

She wished she could read what was in his mind, but she couldn't. She wanted to see sadness, loss, even fear that she would actually call Tyler, but she saw nothing. It was as if he'd turned to stone.

Georgette stared back. "What should I do?" she asked, hoping, praying that Bob would tell her Tyler was completely wrong for her, that he could give her more than Tyler ever could, that his love was worth more than any material goods Tyler could ever provide, and to put the letter through the shredder after all.

"Do what you want. It's your life, and your decision."

Her heart sank. But, contacting Tyler would either give her closure, or a way to start again.

Before she could respond, Bob turned and disappeared into the shop, the door closing harder than usual behind him.

Work couldn't still her mind, she could only think about what could be. At first, she hadn't cared that she'd lost every piece of her past, but it didn't take long before she felt a distinct lack of roots. Bob's roots were a large part of his personality. Seeing Tyler wouldn't restore her relationship with her father, but it would either give her back a piece of who she was, or allow her to make the decision to make the break complete on her own.

Partway into the afternoon, she couldn't stand it anymore. She called Tyler to set up a dinner date.

Bob walked in just as she finished the conversation.

"I see you decided to go."

"Yes," she said, her hand still resting on the phone. "It will bug me if I don't. If it works, fine, and if it doesn't, at least it will give me a sense of closure. We're going out tonight."

He looked down at the floor, not facing her as he spoke. "I guess we won't be making dinner together, then."

"No."

"Then I'll see you Wednesday. Bart and I switched days off this week. I've got tomorrow off, and he's got Thursday off."

"Oh." Her heart sank. Whether things went well or badly, it had comforted her to know that Bob would be there for her the next morning, but it was not to be. She didn't want to wait until Wednesday to see him again. "What about dinner tomorrow?"

He shrugged his shoulders. "Dunno," he mumbled as he turned his head back toward the shop. "I have to get back to work."

"Wait. Didn't you come in here for something?"

He shrugged his shoulders with a grimace. "I forgot what it was. If it was important, it'll come back to me. Have fun tonight."

Georgette watched as Tyler sipped his wine, then spoke to her over the top of the flute. "I don't know how you managed to get in and out of that truck in that dress. I could have picked you up or called a cab."

She smiled weakly. It wasn't the dress that was the hard part. It was the shoes. She hadn't worn heels for so long, her ankles wobbled. When she'd slid out of the truck, she'd nearly fallen down when she landed.

Dinner with Bob every Thursday had been different. She had the money to pay her own way. They both wore jeans, and chose places where a meal didn't cost a whole day's salary.

"Let's just say the truck keeps me humble."

"I'm so glad you decided to come. There are so many things I want to say to you."

She noticed that he hadn't given her any time to say anything that *she* might have wanted to say. He didn't ask her how she was coping, how she liked working for a living or even if she was happy. Even though she was the one wronged, the conversation was still about Tyler.

Bob would have made sure she was comfortable first, and he always let her vent if something was bothering her, even if it had nothing to do with him. Bob always listened before he talked.

"I've missed you, Georgette. I didn't notice until I wasn't seeing you any more how much your smile helped whatever had gone wrong that day. And you always understood what I was talking about when I talked business. No other woman I dated cared much about the workings of my day. They only cared when it meant I couldn't take them where they wanted to go."

Georgette held back a sigh. The alleged apology centered around Tyler. She couldn't believe she was hearing about his dates with other women, *he* was the one who'd set up this "special time."

Bob never talked about other women. The one time she'd asked about a woman he'd dated, he'd quickly changed the subject.

"You're always happy, no matter where we go or what we do."

Every time they'd gone out, it had been to a place of Tyler's choosing. Many times, he'd picked the last place on earth she wanted to be. Tyler's word meant nothing. No matter what he promised, she knew she would never trust him fully, not after he'd betrayed her so badly at the first opportunity for his own gain.

Bob never went back on his word. For a short time, she could tell that Bob wasn't sure if he'd made the right decision to let her move into his garage. But he'd given her his word, and that was final. He was a true man of honor.

"I guess what I'm trying to say is that I think we're a good match. I think it would suit us both to get married."

Georgette choked on her tea. "Married! Are you serious?"

He smiled a nice, corporate businessman's smile. No warmth, no personal connection. It looked as if it was painted on. "Of course I'm serious. We'd both get what we want, and each of us would benefit."

She set the cup on the saucer, before she dropped it and broke it. "How do you know what I want?"

The phony smile stuck to his face, but didn't reach his eyes. "I know you want the good life back. You can't possibly be happy having to work every day and then go home and bury yourself in chores. But if you wanted to keep working, that would be fine with me. I wouldn't even mind if you wanted to go to church every once in a while. It's a noble thing to do, and it looks good, too."

She was so flustered she could barely talk. "What—what about you? Would you go to church with me?" She didn't want him to go to church with her just to sit beside her. She wanted to marry a man who shared her faith. Like Bob.

He shrugged his shoulders. "I would probably go a few times a year, like Christmas, Easter and probably Mother's Day. After we had children and you became a mother, of course."

The thought of having children with Tyler made Georgette gag. Rather than losing the meal that had cost more than the brake job she'd been saving for, she stood. "You know, I have to get up early for work tomorrow. I think it's time to go."

He reached for her hand, but she pulled it away before he made contact.

"Wait, Georgette, there's something else. After you called me, I talked to your father. He wasn't exactly pleased, but I did manage to convince him to take you back. He said he would restore your credit cards and give you back the car. I realize I sprung this on you rather quickly. Moving back home would give you more time to think about it."

She backed up a step, unable to speak. She'd always imagined a proposal would be a little more personal. Even romantic. Fat chance.

Tyler took another sip of his wine and again spoke to her over the glass. "Marriage isn't a bad thing, you know."

Marriage. She still didn't know whether her mother had deserted her two young daughters because she couldn't stay married to a man who treated her badly, or if her mother had been thrown out for not measuring up.

The last time she'd spoken to her sister, Terri had been crying because Byron was cheating on her. Yet Terri stayed in a marriage where there was no love rather than going back to their father's emotional abuse.

She couldn't imagine being married to Tyler, who always thought of himself first.

She wouldn't marry a man like Byron, who'd only married her sister for her assets.

The only man she would ever marry would be Bob.

Georgette froze.

Bob.

She wanted to marry Bob.

She was in love with Bob.

She didn't know when it had happened, but they could talk about anything and everything. They both could get mad and then laugh about it afterward. And then there was the kiss…

He couldn't have kissed her like that if he didn't mean it.

Georgette struggled not to close her eyes at the memory. She'd sure meant it. But she wasn't with Bob now. She was with Tyler.

"I'm really sorry, but this was a mistake. I can't marry you, and I'm certainly not going to go back to living under Daddy's terms and conditions for the sake of a little money." Not that it was a "little money," but she had learned the hard way that it really didn't buy happiness. "Thank you for dinner, it was lovely. In case I never see you again, have a good life, Tyler. I hope you find the woman who will be right for you one day. I know I'm not her."

Georgette drove home as quickly as she could without getting a speeding ticket. When she pulled onto the cement pad beside Bob's car, not a single light was on in his house.

She closed the truck's door as quietly as she could, and retreated into the apartment.

Tonight she wouldn't wake him, and tomorrow during the day, she wouldn't see him because she had to work. But after work she intended to make use of her newfound discovery.

When they were together, Bob only saw "George the Mechanic." Now that she was aware of her own desires for a future with Bob, Adrian's words came back to her, and now she believed them to be true. However, something was holding him back.

Regardless, Georgette smiled to herself as she got ready for bed. Tomorrow things would change, because tomorrow, she had a plan.

Chapter Eighteen

"Hey! George!"

Georgette spun around, then tried to determine who in the crowded mall had called to her.

A man seated on one of the benches next to the planter stood, with a hot dog in one hand and a drink in the other. "What are you doing here?"

"Randy," she said, sighing as she pressed one palm over her heart. "You startled me. I guess you're on your supper break."

"Sorry," he said and nodded as he bit into the hot dog and swallowed. "Is something wrong with Bob?"

"I assume he's fine. He traded days off with Bart, so I think he's at home. Why do you ask?"

"I've never seen you here shopping without him, that's all."

Georgette smiled. She was shopping alone because she didn't want Bob to see her purchases. Not yet. "Actually, this isn't the kind of trip he would enjoy. I'm going to buy some girl stuff. You must know the mall well. Where would be a good place to buy a nice dress?

I don't want to spend too much money, but I want something nice."

"There's a ladies' clothing boutique beside where I work. It must be good. There's always women going out with big bags in their hands. Try that one."

"That's great. I'll do that."

The first thing that caught Georgette's attention was a big sign stating Summer Clearance.

She headed straight for the sale rack of dresses.

A woman a few years older than her approached. "Can I help you?"

"I don't know. I want to wear something special for tonight, but I don't have a lot of money to spend."

She hadn't originally even planned to go to the mall. She'd gone grocery shopping on the way home, and gone way over budget in order to cook Bob a very special meal. She'd already phoned him to invite him over, but how she would serve it would be a surprise. Her plan wouldn't work if she was wearing the same old jeans and T-shirt he saw her in every day. When their supper was in the oven, she'd gone to change into her beloved green dress. Her heart sank when she discovered a big rip in the bottom. She must have caught her heel in the hem when sliding out of her truck after the non-date with Tyler but in the dark outside, she hadn't seen the damage.

"The dress I wanted to wear has a hole in it, so now I have to buy something new. I'm kinda out of time."

The woman smiled. "Then let's find something nice in your price range."

Together they picked out a flattering style that was just on the edge of Georgette's meager budget, which meant her muffler and a few other repairs on her truck would have to wait. Randy was walking into the electronics store next door just as she ran out. He looked down to the bag under her arm, winked and waved as she ran past him and headed back home.

She was just doing up the zipper when she heard a knock on the door. She yanked on a slip, stuffed her jeans and T-shirt into the armoire, ran her fingers through her hair to tidy it, and ran to the door.

Bob's eyes grew as big as saucers when he saw her. "Did I get the day mixed up? I thought you went out with Tyler yesterday."

He took one step backward, but Georgette grabbed his arm to stop him. "I thought that if I can dress up for Tyler, I can certainly dress up for you."

He looked again at the dress, which fitted her to perfection, even though the style wouldn't have been her first choice. It was a deep blue that went well with her eyes, though the top was too low. But she couldn't argue with the price. He cleared his throat, and wiped his palms on his jeans. "Okay... But then I'm really underdressed."

"You're fine. It was supposed to be a surprise."

He glanced to the table, where she'd set a red candle in the center, something Bob's mother had given her, which she thought gave everything a romantic touch.

"Uh... Yeah... I'm surprised."

She led him to the table and sat him down. "I made you something special."

He turned toward the stove expectantly even though everything she was cooking was back in the oven after her secret last-minute errand—except the salad of course. "Why?"

Because I love you, she thought. "Because you deserve a special evening," she said.

According to the clock, everything should be cooked, so she donned the oven mitts and bent over to take the food out of the oven.

When she turned around, Bob's eyes averted quickly to her face and his ears darkened, telling her that when she'd bent over, he'd been watching. If it had been anyone else, she would have smacked him. But since it was Bob, she smiled inwardly, knowing he appreciated the view. That was one of the reasons she'd worn the dress. She gently plated their meal and carried the plates to the table, then set the potato casserole on the trivet, and retrieved the salad from the fridge.

"Wow. Chicken cordon bleu. And this potato casserole is my favorite. How did you know?"

Actually, she'd asked his mother, who had e-mailed the recipe to her at work that afternoon. That extra work meant she'd had to buy the chicken cordon bleu at the supermarket, ready-made. Knowing her skills, though, that was probably for the best. "Let's just say it's my little secret."

"I don't know what to say."

"Then say grace, so we can eat before it gets cold."

He said what she thought might have been the world's shortest prayer of thanks, and dug in to the chicken.

Bob closed his eyes and sighed. "This is so good. You're a better cook than you think."

She had to laugh at that. "Bob, you can still say that after the Great Stir-fry Fire? All right I'll admit it, I bought the chicken already made up."

He savored another morsel and smiled. "Well, you did a fine job of heating it up without a microwave."

She smiled at him, hoping her nervousness didn't

show. Who knew if her hair and makeup would withstand the heat of the small kitchen.

"I made dessert, too." Even though it was just a mixture of pudding, gelatin and whipped cream, she'd still put it together herself.

His eyebrows raised. "I don't understand. Are you going to tell me something bad?" His fork froze halfway to his mouth. "You're not quitting, are you?" His face paled. "You were out with Tyler last night...."

"Yes, I was," Georgette cut in finally. "I'm glad you convinced me to read that letter. It helped me come to a few decisions about my future."

Bob's face paled further. He had a death grip on that poor fork.

She tipped her head and studied him. "Are you feeling okay? Was this a bad night?"

He lowered the fork and dabbed at his mouth with the napkin. "No, I'm fine. I skipped lunch. That must be it. What did you decide?"

"I decided that I was right all along. Tyler is a jerk, and events, as unpleasant as they were, did work out for the best. I also decided that it's about time I started dating."

Bob's eyes flitted to the candle, then to her low-cut dress, and back to her face. "And tonight?"

"Tonight is for you."

His confusion registered in his eyes. She'd been evasive on purpose, for fear of eliciting a decisive but negative response. Tonight, she needed to show him that she no longer wanted to be George. From now on, for Bob, she was going to be Georgette, and not just as an employee either. She wanted to be Mrs. Georgette Delanio.

"Okay..." he muttered, and resumed eating. "So

how was work today? Did that guy say anything about that 4X4?"

"It was more than he thought it would cost, but he seemed happy after I showed him what was wrong with the old oil pump. I explained how if we didn't replace it now, it would cost him double to have to take the engine apart in just a few months again."

"And what about that old station wagon?

She hadn't intended to talk about work, but she couldn't not answer. Although, when the conversation drifted to his motorcycle and what he wanted to do with it, she forgot all about her previous conviction not to talk shop, and lost herself in the discussion of the restoration process.

They spent far more time at the table than she had intended, but then again she hadn't thought to plan beyond the meal. She couldn't even rent a movie, because she no longer had a DVD player. For now, buying one didn't fit into her budget. *Especially* not after buying the dress.

"Can I help with the dishes?"

She looked at the mess on the counter. It wasn't much, but the counter was so small that even a few utensils out of place made it look messy. She was dressed to go out, but her plan to make the evening a romantic event had already taken a dramatic nosedive from all the shop talk.

"Sure. You wash, and I'll dry."

Bob nodded, rolled up his sleeves, and began rinsing the residue off the baking sheet while Georgette spooned the leftover casserole into a plastic container and put it into the fridge. When she turned around, Bob was already up to his elbows in the soapy water, softly humming a song they'd sung at the weekend retreat.

It was no wonder she loved him so much.

By the time the dishes were done, she could no longer hold herself back. She had to touch him. To hold him. To tell him she loved him.

She watched him wring out the dishrag, and just as he began to turn around, Georgette stepped in front of him, with very little distance between them. In order to prevent him from moving away, she rested her hands at the sides of his waist. "Thank you for a lovely evening," she said, surprised at the rough timbre of her own voice.

He smiled down at her. "I think that's my line. You're the one who made supper. Which was great, by the way. Thank you."

"Isn't the way to a man's heart through his stomach?" With that thought in mind, she raised one hand and pressed her palm over his heart. The steady rhythm thumping against her hand was strangely comforting.

He pressed one hand over hers. As he did so, the speed of his heartbeat increased just a little. "George, I don't think this is a good idea."

"Why not?" she asked as she covered his hand with her remaining one.

In a flash, his other hand covered hers, completing the connection. "It just isn't."

She leaned into him, tipping up her chin, making it easy for him to kiss her if he wanted to, because she sure wanted to kiss him. "Then what would be the way to your heart?"

"I…uh…"

Everything she'd learned about how to attract a man flew out the window. She didn't want to play coy or cunning, but she didn't care how it happened, as long as it happened.

She raised herself up on her tiptoes, leaning into him so much she could feel his knuckles digging into her chest and stomach. "Kiss me, Bob," she whispered huskily, her mouth only inches from his.

Time stood still, and just as she began to wish the earth would open and swallow her up, Bob's lips touched hers. It was nothing like the first time. This time, he kissed her as if he couldn't stop.

So, of course, she kissed him right back.

He pulled his hands out from between them, and held her tight as he kissed her again and again until she was breathless and her heart was pounding so hard she knew he had to feel it, because she could certainly feel his heart pounding beneath her palms, which were still trapped between them.

He lifted his mouth from hers, muttered her name, buried his face in her hair then hugged her even closer.

Georgette's heart soared as she pressed her cheek into his chest. A kiss like this could only mean one thing. Confirmation.

"This won't work, you know," he said softly.

She stiffened from head to toe. She couldn't believe he would say such a thing when she was still enclosed in his embrace. "What do you mean?"

"For now, we're both charged. This thing, whatever it is, is new and exciting. But as time goes on, that novelty will wear off and you'll start to feel trapped. I can't offer you what you've left behind. Not even close. You're better off on your own. You should find a man who can treat you the way you'd like to be treated, and then you can live the way you want to live. I've seen it before. It's one thing to marry into money. It's quite another to marry out of it. I don't want you to come to hate me. When I get married, it's going to be for life, just as God dictates."

"You're wrong. I'm finished with that kind of life. Money isn't where true happiness is. It can't even promise stability if there's too much worry about losing it. It can be evil."

"It's not wrong to be rich, George. People get it wrong all the time, but God doesn't say that money is the root of all evil. He says it's the *love* of money that's the root of all evil. It's very different. But the bottom line is that you don't belong here. I won't keep you. It's not right, and I really don't believe you would be happy being stuck here for the next fifty years. I'm a mechanic, and that's all I'll ever be. And I'm okay with that. But you were made for better things."

"But I…" she let her voice trail off. She nearly said she loved him, but she didn't want to beg him to take her, when he was pushing her away.

He released her and stepped back. Ice pervaded her soul.

"I have to go. We rescheduled worship team practice for tonight, and even though Adrian and Celeste won't be there on Sunday, we're still practicing at his house."

"They won't be there?" she echoed weakly.

"They're getting married this weekend, remember? The rehearsal is Thursday night, Friday we have a bunch of setup and other wedding-type stuff to do, and then the wedding is on Saturday. I'll be really busy, so it would be better if you went by yourself, because then at least you can come and go with the rest of the guests."

"Oh, uh, I guess."

He backed up another step. "So I'll see you around, or something."

The door opened and closed before she had a chance to respond.

Georgette refused to break down and cry or throw things. Bob was right. She had been raised better than that. But some things were worth breaking rules for.

Seeing red, she stomped to the door, and kicked it so hard she hurt her toes.

"Love stinks!" she yelled at the top of her voice and limped off to bed. There was breaking the rules, and then there was nearly breaking a foot. There had to be a better way.

Chapter Nineteen

"You may now kiss the bride."

Bob watched his friend kiss his new bride.

Of course he was happy for Adrian and Celeste, but watching them kiss only reminded him of kissing George a few days ago.

It felt like a lifetime ago.

At work nothing had changed, but everything was different.

George had been avoiding him, and he supposed if the situation had been reversed, he would have felt the same. Between the dress, the wonderful dinner and the way she'd initiated their kiss, it was obvious that she had strong feelings for him. That left the decision in his lap. Even though it wasn't what he wanted, he had to back off. He was realistic enough to know that what they had couldn't last a lifetime.

Bob smiled for the cameras as he escorted a bridesmaid down the aisle behind Adrian and Celeste.

He should have been happy, but he wasn't. Watching Adrian and Celeste only reminded him of what he couldn't have.

He couldn't have Georgette.

Bob shook his head, then forced himself to smile for another camera.

For the first time, he'd thought of her by her real name, not her mannish nickname. He didn't know if he could ever look her in the face and think of her as George again.

It was the way she'd inched herself into kissing him, the dress hadn't hurt, either. He loved her so much. She did everything she could to get him to kiss her; when she'd flat out told him to, he could no longer hold himself back. He'd felt a connection between them like nothing he'd experienced in his life. And now, if the dress she'd worn Wednesday night hadn't been enough to send his brain into outer space, tonight she was wearing the very memorable green dress.

Georgette Ecklington was definitely all woman.

Unfortunately, she was too expensive a woman for him.

By the time he was seated at his place at the head table, he felt utterly miserable. He was at a point in his life where he wanted to settle down and get married, and he'd fallen in love with the wrong person.

When everyone else closed their eyes to pray for their meal, Bob prayed for God to help him deal with his situation. The ceremony had kept him busy, and then there were wedding pictures in the park. For twenty minutes, the guests watched a video that Randy had made of Adrian and Celeste's courtship and the time leading up to the wedding, which provided a good comic relief. But, that was over too quickly. They were having dinner now, and before long that would be over, too. Soon, it would be time to mingle with all the guests including Georgette.

Mentally, Bob shook his head. *George*. In the green dress. But she was still George. A mechanic. His employee. A woman who had lived with the best the world could offer, when he could offer nothing.

The woman he loved, and would love until his dying day.

Bob's heart clenched every time someone new started tinkling glasses for the bride and groom to kiss. He couldn't help himself. Every once in a while, he glanced at George. She didn't look as if she was having a better time than he was.

When dinner was over, he made his way around the floor. Without realizing how he got there, he found himself at George's table, where she sat talking with his mother, of all people. The second the two of them noticed him, his mother got up to leave without saying a word. He didn't know if that was good or bad.

"Hi," he mumbled, for lack of anything better to say as he slid into the chair beside George.

"I'm glad you're here," she said, although her voice was anything but cheerful. She sounded as sad as he felt. "I have to talk to you, and I suppose this is as good a time as any. I need to know how much notice to give you."

Bob's heart stopped beating. "Notice?"

"Yes. I think I've found another place to live, and they need to know when I can move in. I assume that the sooner I leave, the better, so you can find a paying renter."

"I don't understand."

"I've also started looking for another job. I haven't found anything yet, but I thought it would be fair to let you know."

His heart nearly stopped, and he had to force himself to breathe. "Do you need more money? I can give you a raise."

She sighed, and something about her looked even more sad than she already was. "This isn't about money. In fact, if the next job I find pays less money, I'll still take it. I can't handle only seeing you at work, and knowing that's all it will ever be. You've shown me how to budget, how to cook and how to take care of a home. I think it's time for me to put all that practice into use and function on my own."

"But—"

She held up one palm to interrupt him. "You suggested it, Bob, not me. I think you know what I want. Without that, it's torture to work with you all day and go home to your garage at night. It's time."

Bob's head spun.

She was leaving.

He'd been telling himself for months that it wouldn't work, and he should have seen this as the solution, but it felt as if his world was coming crashing down around him.

"What about Tyler? And your father?"

She sighed and looked away, staring at a blank spot on the wall. "They will never change, and I've changed too much to go back. I'll keep praying for them, and one day, I'll contact Daddy and see if he's ready to accept me as I am. But until that happens, I guess I'll just keep working and plugging along. I'm not unhappy. In fact, I've been more content in the last few months than I have been at any time in my whole life."

"You say that now, but it hasn't been very long. Life sometimes has a way of beating a person down."

"God is always with me. Hasn't He always been with you?"

"Of course He has."

"What about when you started your business with Bart? Didn't people warn you that it might not work?"

He let out a humorless laugh. "George, we were both nineteen years old and we started out of my parents' garage. Nearly everyone we knew told us it wouldn't work. There were times when Bart and I were the only ones who thought it would. And sometimes we weren't even sure ourselves."

"And what about now? Hasn't God been faithful?"

"Of course."

"I believe God will be faithful to me. I may not always have the biggest and the best, but that doesn't mean I'll be unhappy. I know I'll have struggles. Everyone does. I'll face them, and I'll become stronger. I've just done that, Bob, and I'll do it again."

Bob stared at her, her words finally sinking in. She *had* made it through before.

The bright spot in his day was the minute George arrived at work, and the bright spot in his evening was when they sat down together to eat supper. On the weekends, he even enjoyed doing simple housework with her and then working on his old Harley.

She was the answer to all his prayers for the perfect life partner. If she left, his life would not only be empty, it would be meaningless.

He stood. "Stay with me."

"I can't. It hurts too much. I know it could work between us, but it won't if I'm the only one who believes it."

"But I do believe it. I was wrong." He stood and held out one hand toward her. When she gently put her hand in his, he pulled her to her feet, then cupped her face with his hands. "I'd like you to stay in the garage until we can get married. George, will you marry me? If you're willing to give me a second chance. A second chance for forever."

She rested her palms on his shoulders. "Are you sure?"

"I've never been more sure of anything in my life." He finally knew what he had, and he prayed it wasn't too late for him to keep it.

"Then of course I will," she said, then snuggled closer. *"Ti amo."*

He smiled, and slowly ran one finger down her cheek. "I love you, too. How did you know how to say that in Italian?"

Her cheeks darkened. "Your mother taught me."

Just as Bob leaned down to kiss her, the flash of a camera glared.

He opened his eyes, glanced to the side, and lowered his hands to her shoulders. "Randy," he mumbled.

"Whoo-hoo!" Randy exclaimed, waving his digital camera in the air. His movements stilled, he took one more picture of the two of them gaping at him, did a short two-step dance, twirled around, and sauntered away.

"He's going to be the best man, isn't he?"

Bob sighed. "Yup. I hope you know what you're in for."

George's arms slid around to his back, she tucked her head under his chin and embraced him fully. "I sure do, and I can hardly wait.

* * * * *

Watch for Randy's story,
CHANGING HER HEART,
next in the MEN OF PRAISE *miniseries*
in February 2006.

Dear Reader,

Welcome once again to Faith Community Fellowship!

Many people work hard all their lives. Many of us work too hard, and need to slow down before it's too late. Sometimes we need to work harder than those around us to get what we want, or even what we need. In both these times, often God sends messages, or messengers, in likely and unlikely forms, for our own good, whether we like it, or not.

The hardest part can be meeting in the middle. It is human nature to keep going the same way, just because we know what to expect. I've often heard it said that the greatest fear is the fear of the unknown. In this story, Bob didn't know what it would be like not to work… *hard*. Georgette didn't know what it was like to work at all. Of course, the best place is somewhere in the middle, and I hope you enjoyed the story of how Bob and Georgette met each other, with God's guidance, in that middle ground.

With the closing of *His Uptown Girl* we move next to Randy, who sometimes marches to the beat of a different drummer.

I look forward to seeing you again, when we see what God has in store for Randy.

Until then, may God bless you in your daily journeys.

gail sattler

And now, turn the page
for a sneak preview of
DIE BEFORE NIGHTFALL
by Shirlee McCoy,
part of Steeple Hill's exciting new line,
Love Inspired Suspense!
On sale in September 2005
from Steeple Hill Books.

Chapter One

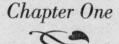

She'd never hung wash out to dry, but that wouldn't keep her from trying. Raven Stevenson eyed the basket of sopping white sheets and the small bucket of clothes pins sitting at her feet. How hard could it be?

Five minutes later she'd managed to trample one sheet into the mud. The other two were hanging, lop-sided and drooping, from the line. "It could be worse, I suppose."

"Could be better, too." A pie in one hand, a grocery bag in the other, Nora Freedman came around the side of the house, her eyes lined with laughter as she eyed the muddy sheet. "Never had to dry laundry the old-fashioned way, I see."

"I'm afraid not. Hopefully it won't take me long to get better at it."

"It won't. You wouldn't believe how many renters have turned away from this property just because I don't have a clothes dryer."

"Their loss. My gain."

Nora beamed at the words. "I knew it, knew the minute I saw you, you were the person for this place. Here, I've brought you a welcome gift. Pecan pie and some things to stock your cupboards."

"You didn't have to—"

"Of course I didn't. I *wanted* to. I'll leave everything in the kitchen. Gotta scoot. Prayer meeting in a half hour. Call me if you need something."

"I will. Thank you."

"See you at church Sunday? You did say you planned to attend Grace Christian?"

The nerves that Raven had held at bay for a week clawed at her stomach. "Yes. I'll see you then."

"I knew it. Just knew this would work out." Then she was gone as quickly as she'd come, her squat, squarish figure disappearing around the corner of the house.

In the wake of her departure the morning silence seemed almost deafening. Raven hummed a tune to block out the emptiness, bending to lift the dirty sheet, her gaze caught and held by a strange print in the barren, muddy earth. A footprint—each toe clearly defined, the arch and heel obvious. Small, but not a child's foot. Someone had walked barefoot through the yard on a day when winter still chilled the air.

Who? Why? Raven searched for another print and found one at the edge of the lawn. From there, a narrow footpath meandered through sparse trees, the prints obvious on earth still wet from last night's rain. She followed the path until it widened and Smith Mountain Lake appeared, vast and blue, the water barely rippling. And there, on a rickety dock that jutted toward the center of the lake, her quarry—white hair, white skin, a bathing suit covering a thin back.

Raven hurried forward. "Are you all right?"

"Thea?" The woman turned, wispy hair settling in a cloud around a face lined with age. "I've been waiting forever. Didn't we agree to meet at ten?"

Ten? It was past noon. Two hours was a long time to sit half clad in a chilly breeze. Raven's concern grew, the nurse in her cataloguing what she saw—pale skin, goose bumps, a slight tremor. "Actually, I'm Raven. I live in the cottage up the hill."

"Not Thea's cottage? She didn't tell me she had guests."

"She probably forgot. Were you planning a swim?"

"Thea and I always swim at this time of year. Though usually it's not quite so cold."

"It *is* chilly today. Here, put this on." Raven slid out of her jacket and placed it around the woman's shoulders.

"Do I know you?"

"No, we haven't met. I'm Raven Stevenson."

"I'm Abigail Montgomery. Abby to my friends."

"It's nice to meet you, Abby. Would you like to join me for tea? I've got a wonderful chamomile up at the house." Raven held out her hand and was relieved when Abby allowed herself to be pulled to her feet.

"Chamomile? It's been years since I've had that."

"Then let's go." Raven linked her arm through Abby's and led her toward the footpath, grimacing as she caught sight of her companion's scraped feet. Another walk through the brambles would only make things worse. "It looks like you've forgotten your shoes."

Abby glanced down at her feet, confusion drawing her brows together. Then she looked at Raven and something shifted behind her eyes as past gave way to present. Raven had seen it many times, knew the moment Abby realized what had happened. She waited a heartbeat, watching as the frail, vague woman transformed into someone stronger and much more aware.

"I've done it again, haven't I?" The words were firm but Abby's eyes reflected her fear.

"Nothing so bad. Just a walk to the lake."

"Dressed in a bathing suit? In…" Her voice trailed off, confusion marring her face once again.

"It's April. A lovely day, but a bit too cold for a swim."

"What was I thinking?" Frustration and despair laced the words.

"You were thinking about summer. Perhaps a summer long ago."

"Do I know you?"

"My name is Raven. I live up the hill at the Freedman cottage."

"Raven. A blackbird. Common. You're more the exotic type I'd think, with that wild hair and flowing dress."

Raven laughed in agreement. "I've been fighting my name my whole life. You're the first to notice."

"Am I? Then I guess I'm not as far gone as I'd thought." Despite the brave words, the tears behind Abby's eyes were obvious, the slight trembling of her jaw giving away her emotions.

Raven let her have the moment. Watched as she took a deep shuddering breath and glanced down at her bathing suit. "I suppose it could be worse. At least I wore clothes this time. Now, tell me, where are we headed?"

"To the cottage for tea."

"Let's go, then."

"Here, slip my shoes on first."

"Oh, I couldn't. What about you?"

"I've got tough skin." Raven slid her feet out of open

heeled sneakers and knelt to help Abby slide her feet into them.

They made their way up the steep incline, Raven's hand steady against Abby's arm. It hurt to see the woman beside her. Hurt to know that a vital, lively woman was being consumed by a disease that would steal her essence and leave nothing behind but an empty shell. Why? It was a question she asked often in her job as a geriatric nurse. There was no answer. At least none that she could find, no matter how hard she prayed for understanding.

"Sometimes it just doesn't happen the way we want."

"What?" Startled, Raven glanced at Abby.

"Life. It doesn't always work out the way we want it to. Sad really. Don't you think?"

Yes. Yes, she did think it was sad. Her own life a sorry testament to the way things could go wrong. Raven wouldn't say as much. Not to Abby with her stiff spine and desperate eyes. Not to anyone. "It can be, yes. But usually good comes from our struggles."

"And just what good will come of me losing my marbles, I'd like to know?"

"We've met each other. That's one good thing."

"That's true. I've got to admit I'm getting tired of not having another woman around the house."

"Do you live alone?"

"Good Heavens, no. I forget things, you know. I live with... I can't seem to remember who's staying with me."

"It's all right. The name will come to you."

Abby gestured to the cottage that was coming into view. "There it is. I haven't been inside in ages. Have you lived here long?"

"I moved in this morning."

"You remind me of the woman who used to live here."

"Do I?"

"Thea. Such a lovely person. It's sad what happened. So sad…"

Take 2 inspirational love stories FREE!

PLUS get a FREE surprise gift!

Mail to Steeple Hill Reader Service™

In U.S.	In Canada
3010 Walden Ave.	P.O. Box 609
P.O. Box 1867	Fort Erie, Ontario
Buffalo, NY 14240-1867	L2A 5X3

YES! Please send me 2 free Love Inspired® novels and my free surprise gift. After receiving them, if I don't wish to receive anymore, I can return the shipping statement marked cancel. If I don't cancel, I will receive 4 brand-new novels every month, before they're available in stores! Bill me at the low price of $4.24 each in the U.S. and $4.74 each in Canada, plus 25¢ shipping and handling and applicable sales tax, if any*. That's the complete price and a savings of over 10% off the cover prices—quite a bargain! I understand that accepting the books and gift places me under no obligation ever to buy any books. I can always return a shipment and cancel at any time. Even if I never buy another book from Steeple Hill, the 2 free books and the surprise gift are mine to keep forever.

113 IDN DZ9M
313 IDN DZ9N

Name	(PLEASE PRINT)	
Address	Apt. No.	
City	State/Prov.	Zip/Postal Code

Not valid to current Love Inspired® subscribers.

Want to try two free books from another series?
Call 1-800-873-8635 or visit www.morefreebooks.com.

* Terms and prices are subject to change without notice. Sales tax applicable in New York. Canadian residents will be charged applicable provincial taxes and GST. All orders subject to approval. Offer limited to one per household.

® are registered trademarks owned and used by the trademark owner and or its licensee.

INTLI04R   ©2004 Steeple Hill